ALL FOR LOVE

A Walker Island Romance, Book 4

Lucy Kevin

ALL FOR LOVE
A Walker Island Romance, Book 4
© 2015 Lucy Kevin

Paige Walker loves her life on Walker Island—teaching dance classes, spending time with her family, and enjoying the beauty all around her. The last thing she's interested in is the spotlight. One fiery brush with that a few years back was more than enough for her! Still, sometimes she can't help but secretly long for more than her quiet life on Walker Island...

TV star Christian Greer has finally gotten his big break starring in a major motion picture. The catch? He needs to learn how to dance like a pro, preferably in a studio far enough from Los Angeles that the paparazzi won't be able to catch any of his stumbles along the way. Walker Island seems like the perfect place to learn to dance and beautiful Paige Walker definitely seems like the perfect teacher.

From their very first lesson, attraction sizzles between them. Christian has never met anyone like Paige and wants their dance to continue beyond the studio. But will he be able to convince her to step into the spotlight with him, and his love, at her side?

CHAPTER ONE

Paige Walker stood in the wings of the Walker Island ballet school's performance area, smiling as she watched her students move gracefully through the brisés and arabesques, échappés and fouettés of *The Nutcracker*. This performance was always one of the highlights of the year for both the school and the community. She could see how excited her students were as they danced their way through the Christmas classic.

She was very proud of her students. They'd all learned so much and had worked so hard this past year. There was nothing she loved more than seeing her students succeed, going from being a little uncoordinated or lacking in confidence to being able to pirouette on stage in front of everyone. It was one of the main reasons Paige devoted so much time to her work at the school.

Dance and her family were the two most

important things in her life.

Turning to look out into the audience, she could see Grams in the front row, as beautiful and engaged as ever. In her early eighties now, Ava Walker still lived in the big family house. She was usually at home when Paige returned in the evenings, often answering emails, or doing fundraising work for the dance studio. Grams was just as devoted to the business now as she had been back when she opened it several decades ago.

Paige's father, William Walker III, whom everyone called Tres, was one of the local high school English teachers, and just like he did every year, he sat beside Grams, silently cheering on his students who were in the ballet production.

She had seen her eldest sister, Emily, backstage just a few minutes ago, looking elegant and composed as always while she helped to keep things organized during the performance. Paige and her sisters referred to Emily as being *bomb-proof*. No matter what was happening, she always managed to look as if nothing was wrong and everything was under control. It was part of what helped make her such a great high school guidance counselor.

Paige's second-oldest sister, Rachel, was also here tonight. Back for the holidays after months of traveling the world with her daughter, Charlotte, and her fiancé, Nicholas, Paige was thrilled to see how blissfully happy all three of them looked. And she was stunned by how much her six-year-old niece had grown in just a few months.

Her sister Morgan was currently backstage, ready with lipstick and mascara for any dancers who might need a touch-up during the performance. Over the holidays, Morgan was taking a much-needed break from work so that she could spend extra time with her fiancé, Brian, and finish planning their upcoming spring wedding. As a professional makeup artist who also had her own makeover show, she had made each and every one of the young ballerinas look beautiful under the lights. Almost as glamorous as Morgan herself. Her star-quality good looks turned heads everywhere she went, but she never seemed to notice.

Last but certainly not least, Paige's youngest sister, Hanna, was also here tonight while her University was on holiday break. A free spirit, Hanna had a style all her own, and in celebration of the season, she'd added Christmassy red and white highlights to her hair. As usual, she was filming everything with one of the many video cameras she used to make her documentaries. Paige smiled at the thought of Hanna and her new husband, Joel Peterson, standing hand in hand at the big upcoming Christmas Eve party. It would mark the first time a Walker and a Peterson had done that in decades.

Paige was thrilled that the whole Walker family had been able to come to tonight's performance—it marked the beginning of their annual Christmas celebrations. After tonight, the dance school would shut down until January, when an excited group of girls would come bouncing in ready to start class again. Ordinarily after this performance, Paige would be on vacation herself, but this year things were going to be a little different.

Actually, teaching a big TV star how to dance is more than a little different, she thought as the performance came to an end and the crowd burst into applause, giving the students a standing ovation.

All thoughts of TV stars fled her mind as several of the girls gestured for Paige to come out onto the stage with them. She waved them back. This was their moment, not hers. Besides, she didn't exactly look her best—her blond hair was tied back in a loose bun that was coming undone, she was wearing her dark-rimmed glasses, and to top it off, she hadn't had time to change out of her leggings before the performance began.

Not that Paige normally thought much about her appearance. Her sisters were the beautiful ones. Morgan, always glamorous with perfect makeup and hair; Emily with her effortless grace; Hanna, always so pretty and artistic looking; and Rachel with the newfound happiness that came from finding true love. Compared to her sisters, Paige knew she was a little bit ordinary. But she didn't worry about it. After all, she liked her life just the way it was.

"Ms. Walker," one of the younger ballerinas

said as she exited the stage, "I think I hurt my foot."

"Let me have a look, Tiffany, and then I'll take you out to your parents."

Paige set to work, gently running her fingers over the little girl's ankle to make sure there was no major damage and then carefully wrapping it with a tensor bandage from the first aid kit. It looked to be only a very light sprain, and Paige was certain that Tiffany would be feeling better by tomorrow.

After Paige took her student out to her parents and explained how to best care for her ankle, Tiffany's mother said, "That was another wonderful performance. I don't know how you do it every year. The kids were terrific."

"They really were, weren't they?" Paige said with a smile. "They're wonderful students. We all have so much fun together."

"Still, I bet you're looking forward to some time off. You deserve it."

After Tiffany and her parents wished Paige a Merry Christmas and she said good night to several other students and their parents, she headed backstage. While she began to clean up, her thoughts shifted again to the work she'd be doing over the holidays this year.

One of the major film studios had decided the time was right for a remake of the 1937 Astaire and Rogers musical *Shall We Dance*, and somehow Paige had managed to let Morgan talk her into helping the leading man with his dance moves. The film was due to start filming in Seattle in early January, which meant the holidays were the only time to get the job done.

To be honest, Paige couldn't imagine why anyone would want to try topping the Fred Astaire and Ginger Rogers original. She remembered sitting curled up on the sofa on a rainy day, watching the movie with her mom, when her mother had suddenly pulled her to her feet.

"Dance with me, sweetie."

They'd broken down every step of every dance in that movie. Her mother had always loved to dance, and Paige had inherited that love completely. Every time she saw the movie, she thought of her mom, and of running through those famous dance sequences in their living room. Ellen Walker had been gone for years now, but Paige still missed her.

When the studio had announced the new female lead, Paige had been impressed, despite her concerns that the remake would ruin her memories of the original. There weren't many ballroom dancers out there better than Liana Haves, and choosing her for the role made Paige think that the studio truly wanted to do justice to the remake.

At least until Morgan had told her who they were casting as the leading man.

"Christian Greer?" Paige had been stunned to find out that the star of the latest hit TV medical drama to break through from the Seattle studios had been chosen to dance in Fred Astaire's shoes.

"You've got to admit," her sister had said, "he's going to be a big draw for the audience."

"You mean a big draw for the fans who just want to drool over their favorite TV doctor," Paige had replied, her heart sinking at the thought that the movie would be ruined by a lead actor who didn't know how to dance.

Okay, so Christian Greer was gorgeous and he would look great in every dance costume—heck, he'd probably look good wearing an old pair of sweats. He was a great actor, too, which everyone seemed to agree on, from the beautiful models who consistently appeared on his arm at Hollywood parties, to Paige's own father, who had settled on *Seattle General Medical* as his favorite TV program.

But none of that meant he could dance. When Paige had pointed that out to Morgan, her sister had shocked her yet again by asking, "Why don't you teach him?"

At the time, Paige had laughed off the absurd suggestion. But thanks to her makeup work with most of the current A-listers and her own hit makeover show, Morgan had plenty of contacts in both the TV and film biz. Paige supposed she shouldn't have been surprised when Morgan came back to her a few days later and said, "Christian thinks it's a great idea. Liana is so busy preparing for the world championships that she won't be able to train him on the dances before they begin shooting. He said himself that he could really use the help. Of course, I told him you're the best dance teacher around." The slightly wicked twinkle in Morgan's eyes made her wonder if dancing lessons were truly the only thing her sister had in mind for Paige and Christian during the week he was on Walker Island.

He was due to arrive tomorrow to start dance training, giving Paige one week to turn him from a total beginner into Fred Astaire. Although, honestly, even with twelve-hour days in the studio, Paige simply didn't know if it was possible. Then again, she thought as she reached down to pick up a set of ballet shoes that one of her students had left behind, how much harder could wrangling one actor for a week be than getting fifty kids to work together perfectly for *The Nutcracker*?

Morgan had already told everyone how nice he was, but Paige was still more than a little nervous about the upcoming week. Thank God she still had another twelve hours to try to get used to the idea of being alone in her dance studio with a big TV star. Especially since it had been quite a while since Paige had been alone with *any* man.

Refusing to let the bad memories of her ex in on what had been such a lovely night, Paige had just stepped around the backstage curtain when she uncharacteristically stumbled. Both her feet and her insides immediately went off-kilter as she realized that Christian Greer was already there, standing in her dance studio, talking with Morgan.

And that he looked even more gorgeous in person than he did on TV.

* * *

Magazines and TV shows always made their stars look better than they did in real life, yet Christian clearly didn't need any help—makeup or otherwise. He was tall and lean, but with obvious strength and muscular definition under his clothes. His black hair was cut in a slightly old-fashioned style that she guessed was a nod to Fred Astaire and the role he would be playing soon. His eyes were deep green, and they seemed to reflect the room around him. And his cheekbones!

Paige had a feeling that they were probably responsible for at least half of *Seattle General Medical's* viewership.

Though her first instinct was to dash backstage to put in her contacts, slap on some makeup, and change clothes, Paige knew there wasn't any point to doing that. After all, it wasn't as if he would see her as anything other than his dance teacher for the week.

"I promise you, Christian," she could hear her sister say as she headed across the room toward them, "everyone is going to *love* having you over to the house for dinner tonight! You're already missing Christmas with your family just to be here for rehearsal. I'd hate knowing you were sitting alone in a hotel restaurant when you could be having a wonderful dinner with all of us."

"Thank you, Morgan. That's really nice of you to offer, but I don't want to impose on your family. Especially since your sister is already going to be working over the holidays just to accommodate my crazy schedule."

"Speaking of my sister..." They both looked over as Paige approached. "Christian, I'd like you to meet Paige."

"Hello, Paige." He gave her a warm—and surprisingly appreciative—smile. "It's a pleasure to finally meet you."

As he took her hand in his, a jolt of awareness shot through her. She'd heard how magnetic he was in person, and of course how attractive. But those stories simply hadn't done him justice. Now she knew why he had been cast in the role that Fred Astaire had made famous: Christian was perfection in every sense of the word.

Meanwhile, here she was looking like something the cat had dragged in.

Turning back to Morgan, he said, "Actually, if the offer is still open, I'd love to come to dinner." He shifted his warm gaze back to Paige. "And maybe if there's time later, we could talk about our plan for next week."

Paige had already known that she would be spending twelve hours a day for the next week dancing cheek to cheek with him. Having him join the family for dinner should be a mere blip on the radar. So then why was her stomach suddenly turning backflips, even though she knew better than to feel the emotions bubbling up inside her? She couldn't let herself turn into the cliché of an island girl falling for a big star. Especially since she'd already been down that road once before, and it had all ended badly, not to mention embarrassingly.

After high school, she'd attended Juilliard and had stupidly fallen hard for Patrice, the premier danseur, after only one gorgeous pas de deux. And then, if that hadn't been bad enough, he'd taken her choreography and left her behind like an old pair of dance shoes. After that experience, she'd decided both her dreams of being a prima ballerina and her dreams of finding Mr. Right were nothing more than foolish childhood imaginings. Looking back, it had all been so predictable, and she was not going to make *that* mistake again.

Which was why she refused to let herself keep blushing like a schoolgirl with a crush or to feel at all embarrassed about looking stained and disheveled from her busy day working with her ballet students. Even if she was standing before the most gorgeous man in the Pacific Northwest.

"It was great meeting you, Christian, and I'm looking forward to working with you. If you'll excuse me, I'd better finish closing things up here. I'll see you later at dinner."

And with that she walked away, trying to pretend that the warmth of Christian's gaze—one that she could still feel trained on her, even without turning to look—hadn't affected her at all.

CHAPTER TWO

Two hours later Christian headed down from his hotel room to his car, which he'd brought over on the ferry from Seattle. It wasn't until he was at the door of the hotel lobby that he realized he hadn't thought to get an address for the Walker house. As he approached the woman at the front desk, he noted that she had the slightly awed look that so many people got around him now that his TV show had taken off in a big way.

"I know this may sound like a bit of a strange question," he said in a friendly tone deliberately meant to put her at ease, "but I've been invited for dinner at the Walker family home and I just realized I don't have their address. You wouldn't happen to know it, would you?"

"Oh that's easy, Mr. Greer. Everyone knows where the Walker house is." She pulled out a small map to give him directions. "In fact, you can walk there from here, if you'd like."

Everyone? That was surprising. But then, the island shared their surname. And it was small enough that locals likely knew where everybody lived. Christian had only just become used to people recognizing him all the time. Had the Walkers had that experience all their lives?

Deciding to head out on foot rather than drive, Christian was soon standing in front of a big, well-tended old house. It wasn't nearly as huge as some of the Hollywood mansions he'd been in, but it looked perfect for raising a large family.

He was just about to knock on the front door when his phone went off. He smiled at the sight of his mother's name on the call display. "Hi, Mom."

"Christian, I was just calling to make sure that you got to the island okay."

"Thanks for checking on me," he said, still smiling. He'd accepted a long time ago that no matter how many birthdays he'd had, his mother would always worry about him. His father had left when Christian was a young boy, and she'd been the best single mother in the world. "Sorry, I meant to phone earlier, but I got caught up on a business call."

"I know you need to prepare for your big new movie role, honey, but I sure am going to miss you this Christmas."

He was going to miss spending Christmas with her, too. It was why he had made sure that his mother would be surrounded by her siblings and their families over the holidays during his absence. Family, he knew, was very important.

"I'm going to miss you, too," he said. "In fact, if dance practice goes well, maybe I could squeeze in—"

His mother cut him off. "If you're going to be the next Fred Astaire, you're going to need every second of those classes you're taking on the island." Her voice softened. "And I just know you're going to do a fabulous job, honey."

"Thanks again for calling, Mom." He thought he heard footsteps coming from inside the house. "I'm about to meet Morgan Walker and her family for dinner, though, so I've got to go."

"You're at Morgan Walker's home?" his mom asked.

"Actually, I'm at the house she grew up in, but I believe her whole family will be there."

"Christian, you know that I am just about her biggest fan ever!" For a moment, she sounded like an awed schoolgirl. One who never missed an episode of Morgan's show. "How could you not tell me this?"

Right then, the front door swung open to reveal Paige standing in the foyer. Wearing dark jeans and a pretty light blue sweater, she looked simply stunning.

She smiled at Christian...at least until she saw the cell phone pressed to his ear. Her smile faded as she gestured that he should come in when he was ready, then she turned and walked away.

"You have to get me Morgan's autograph, Christian," his mom said, now in high gear. "Or, better yet, let me talk to her. You know how much I love her show." When he didn't answer right away, his mother continued with, "I'm sure she won't mind. She seems so nice on TV, and if her family is anything like her, they'll all be just as nice, won't they?"

Christian couldn't help but think about Paige. Of how fresh and pretty she'd looked back at the theater. And the smile she'd given him just now before it had faded. "Yes," he agreed. "Yes, they are very nice."

Morgan walked into the foyer a few moments later, smiling in greeting. "Hold on a second, Mom." Covering the phone with one hand, he said, "Morgan, I'm sorry to do this in the middle of a family occasion, but would you mind speaking to my mother for a few moments? She's a big fan."

Morgan laughed at that. "Your mother's a big fan of mine?"

"Huge."

But Morgan had already reached for the phone and was saying, "Hello, Ms. Greer. Angie, of course…no, it's no problem. It's absolutely lovely to get to speak to you."

Christian listened as Morgan laughed at something his mother said. Probably some story about him as a kid. Like all mothers, she tended to come out with those at exactly the moments when they would be the most embarrassing. Eventually, Morgan said good-bye to his mom and handed the phone back to him.

"Now, honey," his mother said, "you will

make sure to get Morgan's autograph for me, won't you? You won't forget?"

"No, Mom, I won't forget. I love you. I'll call you later." He hung up and turned back to Morgan. "Can I ask one more favor? Can I get your autograph for her before I leave tonight?"

"Absolutely. I'm so flattered." Christian followed Morgan into a large living room filled with people. "Now that I've chatted with your mom, come meet my father, Tres. He's *your* biggest fan."

"It's great to meet you, Christian," Tres said as he shook Christian's hand. "Thanks for joining us for dinner."

"The pleasure is all mine."

The Walker family was very warm and welcoming, if a little on the large side. He was wondering where Paige had disappeared to when Morgan began to introduce him to everyone else. In addition to her father and Paige, there were three other Walker sisters and an assortment of boyfriends and husbands, as well as their grandmother, Ava, whom everyone called Grams. Christian was definitely going to have to be on his game to keep all the names straight tonight.

As they all began to take their places at the large dining table, he was glad to see that he had been seated next to Paige. Very glad.

She wasn't anything like the models and actresses he spent so much time around. No doubt that was part of the reason he wanted to get to know her better. But it wasn't nearly the entire reason. Nor was the fact that they needed to get along so that they would be dancing well together by the time the studio sent an entertainment news crew to the island for a publicity shoot.

No, it was simply that from the very first moment he'd seen Paige in the dance studio, his heart had all but stopped in his chest.

She was beautiful. Breathtakingly, heart-stoppingly beautiful. The kind of beauty Christian thought he ought to be used to after spending years around some of the best-looking actresses in television. Yet, next to Paige, none of those women measured up. Paige had the same blond hair and elegantly crafted features as Morgan, but there was something else there, too. Something that made her look astonishing even in simple dance leggings and glasses.

What *was* it about her? Her porcelain skin? Her innate poise and elegance? Her sky-blue eyes? Christian could certainly think of several co-stars who would happily sell their souls for looks as perfect as Paige's.

Maybe that was a part of it, too. There were plenty of beautiful people in Hollywood, and at the TV studios in Seattle, but few, if any of them, seemed so sweet, or to possess such a sense of decency and gentleness. None of the actresses he knew, for example, would have ever worn dance leggings and a ponytail backstage during a show. On the contrary, they would have been busy making sure that the whole occasion was about them. Whereas Paige had quite obviously wanted to make sure that everything ran as smoothly as possible for the kids. He'd even spotted her backstage, helping out a girl who'd hurt her foot.

Finally, Paige came back into the living room. And as he held out her seat for her—her eyes going wide as she realized she was going to be sitting next to him throughout dinner—he suddenly couldn't help but wonder if this week in Walker Island would change his life forever.

CHAPTER THREE

"Is it true that Jimmy Zhang actually gets faint at the sight of blood?" Paige's father asked Christian.

"You really are a fan of the show if you know about that, Tres," Christian replied with a smile. "The first week we were shooting, it looked like he might have to quit the show, because even though it's fake blood it looks pretty darn real. But he's such a great actor that the writers came up with the idea of making his character an infectious-diseases specialist who can't stand to look at blood, or anything even the slightest bit gross. Of course, by that point Jimmy had spent the week training himself to get over it."

Paige nibbled at her food, barely tasting it, though she'd been starved by the time she'd left the dance studio. She was surprised to note just how effortlessly charming and gracious Christian was as he made her father laugh with the insider information about the TV show before turning to speak to her grandmother.

"I'm sure I've seen you somewhere before, Ava."

"I bet you say that to all the girls, dear," her grandmother replied with a twinkle in her eyes.

Christian laughed, before saying, "I've just remembered, there was a documentary about the island, wasn't there? I caught it at Sundance."

"The documentary was mostly about Hanna and Joel," Grams insisted. "Although I do seem to be getting quite a bit of fan mail. What do you do with your fan mail, Christian?"

"It's hard to stay on top of it," Christian admitted, "but I figure that if they can take the time to write to me, I can take the time to reply. And it helps that a lot of people are getting in touch through social media these days. It means I can keep the conversation going."

Yet again, Paige was surprised by his response. She'd expected him to say that he had people to take care of his pesky fans. After all, he was a really famous TV star. Surely he had assistants for that and for everything else, too.

Then again, when she'd seen him standing on the front step, hadn't she been wrong to assume he was talking to his agent about some new big-money role? Who would have guessed that he would be talking to his mother? And that she would be putting him on the grill about getting Morgan's autograph. He'd sounded like anyone who was trying to please their mother.

It had been kind of cute, actually.

"I've noticed that same thing ever since Michael got me online. It's amazing the way we all end up having a big group conversation," Grams said. "I'm also amazed that people from the strangest places seem to want to ask me about my dancing back when I was young."

"So, dancing runs in the family?"

Paige noted that he seemed genuinely content to listen as Grams explained how she had worked as a dancer in Seattle and how their grandfather had been so supportive when she'd wanted to start the dance school here on the island.

"If Paige has any trouble with you, perhaps you'll find me taking over your dance instruction," Grams joked.

Christian looked over at Paige then, and her breath caught in her throat when she realized how deep and intense his gaze was. He hadn't looked at anyone else that way tonight, she realized.

Only her.

"I don't plan on giving Paige any problems beyond my two left feet. Hopefully, I'll end up being the best dance student she's ever had."

Paige had heard a few horror stories from Morgan about actors who wouldn't follow direction or who didn't seem to understand that they had to make some kind of effort beyond looking pretty. But she knew she needed to at least try to give Christian the benefit of the doubt despite the fact that, on the surface with his standard red carpet shots and paparazzi snaps, everything about him said typical A-list type.

"I'm glad to hear you're excited about getting started with our lessons," she said softly. When he smiled at her, the heat in his gaze had her nearly stuttering on her next far-too-true words. "I am, too."

A short while later, as the plates were being cleared away to make room for dessert, Christian asked, "Would you excuse me for a moment? I need to make one quick phone call."

"Your mother again?" Morgan joked.

"Actually, it's my nephew's birthday tomorrow, and since I know he'll be busy with his friends all day, I figure tonight is my best chance to get him to pick up the phone so that I can wish him a happy birthday."

Paige could practically hear her sisters sigh at how sweet that was. Heck, she was barely managing to hold back her own sigh at this point.

In an effort to think about something—or someone—other than Christian and how great he'd been all night, Paige asked Rachel and her daughter, Charlotte, about their recent experiences surfing off Bondi Beach in Australia. Paige loved the way Charlotte talked her usual enthusiastic million miles an hour as she explained all about how she'd quickly managed to learn to stand up on her surfboard and was now an even better surfer than her mom.

"It sounds amazing," Paige told them, and it

did. In Nicholas, her sister had not only found a man who loved her more than anything, she'd also found a whole new, exciting life for her and Charlotte that had both of them sparkling with happiness.

"Nicholas is *really* famous," Charlotte informed her. "Everyone always wants to say hello and get his autograph. And mine and mommy's, too, now that we're a part of his TV show."

Paige stroked a hand over her niece's hair as she asked her sister, "Do you ever find that it gets a bit much, with people always recognizing Nicholas and now both of you, too?"

"They're mostly very sweet about it," Rachel assured her. "Besides, he's so good with his fans and deserves the attention."

"I'm glad to hear that," Paige said, before laughing and adding, "although you know me, I just can't see why anyone would want to be famous."

"You can't?" Christian asked as he re-entered the dining room.

Just looking at his handsome face had Paige's mind going blank for a moment before she managed to reply, "People coming up to me in the street?" She grimaced. "I would hate that."

"Morgan doesn't have a problem with it," Rachel pointed out. "And Grams is enjoying all the attention she's been getting thanks to Hanna's documentary."

"Yes, well, Morgan was always meant for the

spotlight, and Grams used to be a dancer. They're both used to it." All that attention would be absolute purgatory for Paige.

"But you're a dancer, Paige," Christian commented. "So aren't you used to being in the spotlight, too?"

"No, I'm a dance *teacher.* It's not the same as performing." To deflect his gaze that seemed to see too deeply into her, Paige said, "Brian is also a teacher. He teaches science at the high school and is also the football coach."

"I've always wondered what it must be like to be a teacher," Christian said to Morgan's fiancé.

"It's what I always wanted to do," Brian told him. "Although I'm sure it can't be any harder than your job. I've seen Morgan working."

"I think her job is a little harder than acting, to be honest," he said modestly. "Mostly, I just memorize my lines, stand around until they're ready to start the scene, and then hit my mark."

"But you love it, don't you?" Emily guessed.

"I do," Christian replied with a smile for Paige's oldest sister. "Which is good, because I'm not sure that I'd be much good at anything else."

"That's how I've always felt about being a guidance counselor. Even as a little girl, I used to want to help everyone plan out their lives," she said with a laugh.

"It must be so rewarding watching the kids you've worked with go on to succeed in life."

"It really is," Emily agreed. As Paige watched, Christian easily got Emily talking about her favorite students and how much she loved helping them figure out their passion and then go for it.

"Your grandfather opened the school, didn't he?"

"You've done your research, haven't you?" Paige could tell Emily was impressed.

"I always like to know something about the places I'm going to be spending time."

Christian continued to work his way around the table, asking several questions about what Hanna was filming at the moment for her newest documentary. Inevitably, they got into a discussion about different ways of shooting scenes and the way Hanna would want to change some of the camera angles if she were directing *Seattle General Medical*.

"Sometimes it seems like they're trying to do clever things, going for that reality TV look, but it seems like those things tend to date rather quickly," Hanna said. "I wonder if they'd be better off doing more of the simple shots that give the scene time to breathe. Especially since your show is more about the acting and the story than trying to compress action with the camera."

It was amazing how easily everyone in her family was opening up to him, Paige thought. And when Christian shifted his gaze to her, yet again it struck her that even just the way he looked at her was undeniably sexy, and full of male appreciation.

Not that any of that mattered, of course. The

two of them would be the worst couple in history, with one needing the spotlight and the other absolutely abhorring it.

"Ever since I've taken on this role," he said to her, "people have been telling me how much dance technique I'll need to absorb. But I think what I'm missing most of all is the philosophy of dancing. What dancing means to people. And why dancers are so passionate about doing it."

For Paige, dance was *everything.* Dance was the sense of freedom it gave her, even when she was doing precise pre-determined movements. Dance was being able to express feelings with her body that were so much harder to say with words. Dance was beauty, emotion, and a gently flowing power all at once.

But how could she say that to Christian Greer? Especially while they were at dinner with her entire family?

"I've always loved to dance," she finally said in a soft voice. "It's a part of me that I don't think I could live without."

"They all danced young," Tres added, "but Paige was the only one who stuck with it and followed in my mother's footsteps."

From the way Christian looked at her then, she thought he might be about to reach for her. Maybe to touch her hand or stroke her cheek. And it was the realization of how badly she wanted him to do that that had her jumping up out of her seat and saying, "Excuse me, I'd better go get dessert for everyone."

CHAPTER FOUR

Christian knew he should let Paige disappear into the kitchen to let the heat that was growing between them cool down. But he couldn't remember the last time he'd been this intrigued by a woman. One who came from such a great family but was so different from all of the people she was related to at the same time.

What, he wanted to know, had shaped Paige into the woman she was today? Ava had obviously helped raise all of the Walker girls, but Paige was the only one who had followed in her dancing footsteps. At least part of the way, into teaching.

Was there any part of Paige that longed to be on stage performing? Or was the spotlight truly that horrible to her?

And if so, why?

"I'll go and give Paige a hand," Christian said, standing.

"You're our guest," Emily said, starting to stand up herself. "I'll go."

"I'd really like to help," Christian insisted. And he also desperately wanted a few moments alone with Paige.

It looked as if Emily might be about to argue further, but Christian was used to working with directors who wanted to take charge of everything and was already halfway to the kitchen to help Paige. Out of the corner of his eye, he saw Emily sit back down to resume her conversation with Michael.

Paige was just picking up a platter of meringues in the kitchen when he all but crashed into her. He ended up having to grab the tray, his hands clasping over hers, so that both they, and the desserts, wouldn't go toppling over on the floor.

"Christian, what are you doing in here? You should be back in the dining room, talking to my dad, or to Grams, or—"

"Your family is great, but I'd rather find out more about what makes you tick. I meant it, you know, when I said that I wanted to understand why you love dancing so much." Paige looked as if she didn't quite believe he could possibly be that interested in her.

"I..." Whatever she'd been able to say fell away as their eyes met and held. Even though he knew there were nearly a dozen people in the dining room just behind him, in that moment Christian felt like they were the only two people in the world.

She licked her lips, drawing his focus down to her soft and very sweet-looking mouth before she said, "We should get this dessert out to the dining room before there's a revolt."

It was a distraction, and an obvious one, but Christian knew better than to try to push her too much tonight. Especially with her entire family there. Carefully moving his hands from hers, Christian opened the door to the dining room so that she could carry in the tray of luscious dessert.

But once they were seated at the table again and the desserts had been handed around, Christian realized he just couldn't let it go. "Are you in charge of the big performances with the kids every year at the dance studio?"

"I am, although *The Nutcracker* is our biggest show of the year by far. Hanna," she said as she turned to her younger sister, "why don't you tell Christian about the performance you filmed last year?"

As Hanna regaled everyone with amusing stories about the filming of last year's show, Christian listened attentively, even though what he really wanted was to get back to talking with Paige.

Unfortunately, the perfect opportunity never materialized. Tres was keen to know about the way the next season of *Seattle General Medical* was going to play out. Morgan wanted to catch up on a couple of former clients of hers who were also on his show. Even Rachel's little girl, Charlotte, wanted to explain her idea for a movie—a really cute idea that involved more monsters and spaceships than the average summer blockbuster.

"Time to head home and go to bed now, sweetie," Rachel said, picking her daughter up when she'd finally seemed to run out of steam.

And somehow Paige had again managed to remain in the background throughout. She was, he'd noted tonight, a master of doing that.

"Thank you so much to all of you for the very warm welcome to the island. I should probably be getting back myself. After all, I'm going to need plenty of sleep if I'm going to be ready for a good long day of dancing with Paige tomorrow. And since I managed to make a couple of wrong turns getting here on foot, I should probably plan on some extra time to get lost on the way back, too."

"Why don't you walk him back, Paige?" Ava suggested as she hugged Christian good night. "I'm sure you'll have plenty to talk about, and you can make the arrangements for tomorrow."

"Grams..." Paige began, but then she nodded and even gave him a small smile. She grabbed a coat and her purse and led the way outside.

"It's so much quieter than Seattle," Christian observed as they headed toward the main road. Christian could see the lights of the harbor shining in the distance and a few small pleasure craft at anchor in the bay.

"Is that a bad thing?"

"No, not at all. It's just that when you're used to living in the city, you really notice the difference when you come to a place like Walker Island." In Seattle, there would have been plenty of people still out and about, going out to dinner, or to the theater, or to any number of other events. There were certainly tourists and islanders enjoying similar things here, but on a much smaller scale—and with the stars almost impossibly big and bright as they twinkled from the dark sky above.

"Your hotel is this way," Paige said, leading him down the road into the center of town.

"Once I'm at the hotel," Christian said as a thought occurred to him, "it will mean you'll have to walk back alone. Are you sure you'll be okay?"

Paige waved away his concern. "Walker Island is really safe."

"Especially for you, I'd guess," Christian said, suddenly distracted by the scent of Paige's perfume. It was a subtle, beautifully delicate scent.

Paige looked over at him, a question in her eyes. "Why especially for me?"

"You're a Walker, and I'm guessing that everyone here must know you. It's a little like being famous, isn't it?"

"I guess so." Paige didn't look as if she much liked that idea. "But I try not to think about it too much. Besides, being 'famous' here just because I am a Walker isn't the same as if I'd done something important."

He was silent for a minute before he asked, "Am I saying all the wrong things?"

She stopped walking to stare at him, genuinely surprised, "No. Why would you say that?"

"It's just that when I ask you anything personal, like why you still dance, you change the subject. And now you seem to be doing it again after I asked you about living here. I hope you'll believe me when I say that I'm not just some actor trying to figure out the motivation for his part."

Paige didn't say anything for a few moments, and he got the sense that she was trying to make up her mind about whether to believe him or not. Finally, she reached into her small purse and took out a photograph of a woman dancing. At first he thought it was Paige in the middle of a pirouette. But after staring at it for a little while longer, he realized the picture had obviously been taken many years ago. The resemblance between Paige and the dancer in the photograph was so strong that it was no wonder he was momentarily confused.

"Is this your mom?"

Paige nodded. "She died a long time ago."

"I'm so sorry, Paige." He hadn't wanted to make her unhappy by bringing up painful memories. But before he could tell her that, she continued speaking.

"Mom loved to dance. Grams taught us in the studio, but I also learned to dance from my mom.

At home. In the backyard. All the time, really. She was so beautiful when she danced. This is how I always remember her, and it always felt like we were closest when we were going through routines or she was helping me work out some steps I couldn't quite get. She'd be so happy when it all came together. We both would." Paige was silent for a moment before adding, "She used to dance with my father, too. I don't think I've seen him dance since she died."

Christian was used to watching people and trying to figure out what made them tick. It was what all actors did. But with Paige, he wasn't watching from a distance. Rather, he swore he could not only feel her pain within himself, but all the joy from her mother's love, as well. It was easy to see just how much Paige's mother had meant to her.

And just how private a moment she was sharing with him.

"You dance because of your mom, don't you?"

"She had so much strength, so much grace. And when I'm dancing in the middle of the music, it feels as if I can touch that." She gazed down at the photo with such emotion that he nearly gave in to reaching out to put his arms around her, just the way he'd wanted to earlier in the evening. "It's as if I'm dancing with her again."

As if she suddenly felt she'd said too much, she shook her head as if to clear it and put the photo back in her purse and began walking again. "Your hotel's just down this way."

Christian followed her, but the truth was that he didn't want this walk to end. Just the two of them, out on a beautiful island evening, was simply wonderful. One of the best nights he'd ever had, actually.

Now it was his turn to shake his head as if to clear it. It had been barely three hours since he'd first met Paige, and already he was feeling...

Well, he wasn't yet sure that he could put a name to what he was feeling. Nor did he know why it felt so good having been welcomed so completely into the Walker family in such a short space of time.

As they approached the front steps of the hotel, he knew kissing Paige good night would be completely inappropriate. Even asking her out on a date would be too much, too soon, given the way she'd kept her distance from him most of the night.

Still, he couldn't help but move a little closer as he said, "Thank you for showing me the way back. And for agreeing to teach me to dance when you should be spending the Christmas holiday with your family."

"Don't thank me yet," she responded, and he was glad to see that all traces of her earlier sadness from when they'd looked at her mother's photo were gone now. "I've got a week to turn you into the closest thing to Fred Astaire there's been since the original movie came out. I'll see you at six tomorrow morning at the dance studio."

"Six in the morning?" He was used to having to get to the set early, but that seemed like an awfully early time to get up and dance.

Paige smiled at him then, a hint of wickedness in her eyes, as she said, "I thought I'd take it easy on you for our first day." Then she turned and headed back home. "See you soon."

* * *

Christian was grinning as he walked into the hotel through the impressive front entrance. "Good evening, Mr. Greer," the woman behind the front desk said. "You look as if you've had a pleasant evening."

"As a matter of fact, I have. A nice home-cooked meal and a walk to the hotel along the waterfront was the perfect way to spend my first night on the island."

"I hope the rest of your stay is equally pleasant. And be sure to let me know if we can do anything here at the hotel to make you more comfortable."

As he made his way up to his room, he reflected on the past few hours. It was hard to find fault with anything tonight. Dinner was great, and the Walkers were wonderful. Family was the most important thing in the world to Christian, and the Walkers were a large family that was both close-knit and welcoming, willing to accept a total stranger into their ranks for the evening.

Closing his hotel room door behind him, he tried his best to pin down the feelings he'd had as he and Paige had walked together in the moonlight. Happiness. Warmth. A longing to spend all night beneath the moonlight getting to know everything he could about Paige. And desire, too. So much that it stunned him how much he'd wanted to kiss her.

Was this what love at first sight felt like?

Christian had always assumed love at first sight happened only in the movies, and that it couldn't happen in real life. But suddenly, he wasn't so sure about that anymore. At the very least, he planned to do everything he could to get to know Paige Walker better.

But first, he pulled out his cell phone and set his alarm...for five in the morning.

CHAPTER FIVE

Paige arrived at the dance studio at a quarter to six the next morning, quickly checking her email and forwarding several business matters to Grams. Paige managed a lot of the business of running the studio, but it was still her grandmother's school, and Ava liked to be involved in the important decisions. Paige took a moment to make sure that there were plenty of snacks in the office in case Christian got hungry before lunch.

She took a moment to stand in the middle of the studio, mirrors on every side reflecting her back to herself from every angle. It was amazing how empty a dance studio could feel with no one here. There was a small stand on one side to hold the stereo, a few mats rolled up in one corner, and a barre along one wall. Other than that, it was just a big rectangular box. One that they would fill up with work, sweat, and dance...and that would soon contain nothing but her and Christian Greer, reflected in those mirrored walls.

At five minutes to six, the buzzer for the front door sounded. Paige was impressed with how prompt he was. She didn't imagine most big stars would willingly get up so early on a dark cold winter morning. And when she went to unlock the door, she couldn't believe just how good-looking he managed to be at this time of the day. The sun hadn't even risen yet, but there he was, standing in workout clothes, holding a small sports bag, looking amazing.

"Good morning, Christian." As Paige opened the door for him, she had to ask, "How do you manage to look so eager first thing in the morning?"

"I'm used to it. Movies start shooting at all kinds of hours, especially when the director decides he wants the sun rising in the background of the shot." Christian smiled at her then, and she swore the heat in the studio went up ten degrees. "Plus, I'm looking forward to working with a great teacher."

This morning Paige had made more of an effort with her appearance than she usually did, telling herself all the while that it was because she wanted to make sure Christian knew she was taking their lesson seriously...not because she wanted him to notice her as a woman. But despite her dark leotard, tights, and a short gauzy wrap skirt, there was only so much you could do wearing dance clothes. And when she found herself uncomfortably aware of the way the leotard clung to her curves, she silently reminded herself that Christian wasn't there to look at her, he was there for dance lessons.

Thankfully, he was enthusiastic about learning to dance. Still, she was more than a little worried, given that Fred Astaire and his legacy were still very important in the world of dance. The idea of doing a remake of *Shall We Dance* was tough enough. But the thought of the film, and Christian's role in it, being unsuccessful because she hadn't been able to get him up to the required standards had already made her lose sleep.

As if he could read her mind, he said, "Before we begin, I want you to know I understand that Fred Astaire is the father of dance on TV and in the movies. I know how much he did for the craft and all about his career in stage musicals before he came to film. He is an icon, and I promise you, Paige, I want to do him justice."

"I do, too."

As they stood alone with each other in the studio, the island still dark and sleepy outside, she felt a connection to him that stunned her now even more than it had last night.

Work, she reminded herself. They were here to work on his dance skills, not for her to moon over him like every other woman on the planet.

Forcing herself to focus, Paige started the lesson with some warm-ups. Nothing difficult. Just simple, fundamental movements. They got about ten minutes into the lesson when

Christian's phone went off. To his credit, he ignored it, and Paige did, too.

She continued to focus on teaching him the basic movements. If she could get him to the stage where he could do these correctly, then the movie's choreographer would have a much easier time getting him to do the exacting choreography—especially since he would be paired with a pro like Liana Haves.

That was what she told herself, anyway. Yet it was hard to ignore the fact that these drills didn't involve touching. Because, after the way she'd reacted to Christian time and time again—with both butterflies taking flight and fireworks going off inside her every time he so much as stared into her eyes—she wanted to keep the touching part to a minimum. She knew she would eventually have to show him a dance hold, but not yet. Rather than behave like Ginger Rogers, she was just going to have to be more like Hermes Pan, the choreographer who'd stood at the sidelines shouting instructions.

As the lesson progressed, Christian's phone rang a few more times, but he continued to ignore all the calls, focusing intently on Paige's directions and trying hard to do what she asked.

"You're lifting your shoulders," she reminded him again.

He relaxed his shoulders, but the tension moved elsewhere, making even that gorgeous body of his seem subtly off-kilter. Plus, a few minutes later, his shoulders were tense again anyway.

"Let's take a quick break," she suggested. "There's water over there, and you can also go find out who's been calling you."

While he did that, she went into the storage area at the back of the studio to grab her all-purpose cure-all to help correct shoulders that were out of alignment—the mop they used to clean the floors. By the time she came back, he had put both his phone and the water bottle down.

"This should help you to remember what the right posture feels like," Paige explained as she put it across his shoulders and showed him how she wanted him to hold on to it. "Now, again, from the beginning."

When he started over, she was both relieved and impressed to find that he could remember dance steps as easily as he could learn his lines. Now, they just had to work on polishing them. Unfortunately, once he put down the mop, after a few minutes his shoulders started to go their own sweet way once more. Even when she reminded him, his correct posture lasted only until the distraction of another missed phone call.

Wondering why he wouldn't just turn it off, she pressed on, switching up the exercises, working on the details for hours. Hours filled with mistakes and a huge amount of effort on both their parts, along with continual interruptions from his phone in the corner. Still, though he was having trouble nailing precisely what she was asking him to do, he didn't whine, nor did he complain when she asked him to repeat things over and over again. He obviously had excellent stamina and kept going until his T-shirt was plastered to the muscles of his torso in a way that was impossible for the woman inside of her to ignore.

"You need to rise from the balls of your feet," she said, but even though he tried to follow her directions and needed to be floating over the floor with grace and elegance, he seemed to sink farther down into it with every step, rooting himself in place. It was movement more suitable for martial arts training than for dancing. Maybe, it occurred to her, that was where he'd picked up the habit. Paige could easily imagine Christian doing fight training for some movie or other. Probably looking very good while he did it, too.

Now, if only she could imagine him dancing. Somehow, he made everything else look easy, but this...

Making sure to hold back any sound of frustration, she said, "Why don't we take another break for ten minutes?"

The truth was that she needed a break as much as he did. Not from the dancing. After all, she was used to being on her feet all day with students and showing them by example. Right now, it was more that she needed to rethink her strategy. What she was doing obviously wasn't working. She simply wasn't getting through to him.

Fortunately, she knew exactly who she needed to talk to about it. Closing her office door, she rang her grandmother up at the house.

"How are things going with Christian, honey?"

Paige kept her voice low as she said, "That's actually why I'm calling, Grams. I've got him doing basic exercises, and he's trying really hard, but it's just not coming together."

"Well, you knew there would be a lot of work when you agreed to take on someone who hasn't danced before," Grams pointed out in a gentle voice. "Tell me, how are things coming along when you're actually dancing with him? A new partner changes things, and that might be part of it."

Paige swallowed hard. "I haven't actually danced with him yet."

"You haven't? Why ever not?"

"I just...I wanted to concentrate on getting the exercises right."

Her grandmother made a small sound of disbelief. "That isn't all of it, is it, Paige?"

"No," she admitted, "it isn't. I've been putting that part of our lessons off."

"Sweetie, you're his dance teacher. You know you need to touch him."

Paige knew her grandmother was right, of course. She'd avoided partnering with him all day, thinking that the exercises would be enough. But they weren't. Of course they weren't. How could they be?

She was acting like a love-struck teenager, and she needed to pull herself together.

Paige felt terribly guilty that she had effectively wasted an entire morning, all because she hadn't wanted Christian to find out how much his presence unsettled her. She'd wanted to avoid appearing like the kind of weak, simpering fan he probably saw every single day of his life. But, in doing that, she'd held back from giving her student the best possible lesson.

"You're a fabulous teacher, Paige," her grandmother continued. "The best I've ever known. If anyone can do this, you can."

Paige hung up the phone, trying to believe what Grams had just said—that if anyone could turn Christian into a serious dancer, she could.

Of course, to do that she was going to have to actually touch him.

By the time Paige walked back into the main part of the studio, she was surprised to find him sitting against the wall with his head in his hands.

"Christian?" He looked up, starting to push himself to his feet. She cut that short by moving to sit down beside him. Sitting there like that, he looked so vulnerable. It was such a contrast to the easy strength that he usually possessed.

"It looks like you were right. I'm no Fred Astaire."

"No one is," Paige pointed out. "And you've only been learning for one day."

She was willing to bet that just about everything else came easily to Christian, from his success on TV shows to all the things that were connected with that. Fame, fortune, women. She could imagine how hard struggling with learning to dance must be for him.

"The big entertainment shows are going to be coming in to film us practicing at the end of the week." The strain in Christian's voice was crystal clear. "They'll be only too happy to run with a story about how I'm going to butcher Fred Astaire's classic role."

"Then we just need to work even harder. You'll get it," Paige assured him, "and when you do, you'll wonder why it seemed so hard at first. But it's going to take lots more focus. From both of us."

Almost as if to punctuate their need for focus, the sound of a phone ringing came from Christian's sports bag, a distinctly un-macho set of tinkling bells. He winced, but this time he finally got up to take the call.

"Hi. Yes, it's fine. No, I haven't forgotten, I promise. Yes, I know you do. Tell them I do, too. I'll see you all soon." He turned to Paige. "What time does FedEx close on the island?"

"Five o'clock, but we've still got so much to do."

"I know, and I'm sorry. It's just...wherever I go, I try to send something back to my two nieces when I get there. The tackier, the better, generally. That was my sister, reminding me that I should be spending Christmas with them rather than wandering off preparing for my new role. So

I figure I've got between now and the time FedEx closes to find something suitably touristy to make up for it. At least it will remind them that I'm thinking of them." He ran a hand over his face. "I know it probably sounds like I'm making excuses not to practice—"

"No, it doesn't sound like that at all. We've had a long day, and I know how important family is." She paused for a moment before deciding to tell him, "After my mother died, my father traveled a lot, almost as if being on Walker Island hurt him too much. But he never wanted us to think that he'd forgotten us, so he would send us things from all around the world. Little things. Shells he'd found on a tropical beach. Pictures of places he'd gone with his students. So I know how important tacky souvenirs can be for children. They show you're thinking of them even when you're away."

"Thank you for understanding," Christian said. "I really didn't want to quit practice early on my first day."

Paige looked at his sweat-soaked form. "I think you've been working hard enough for a first day, and I know we're absolutely going to kill it tomorrow. So go on. The FedEx office closes in an hour, which means that you should have just enough time to find some really tacky gifts at one of the little tourist shops on the same stretch of downtown."

"Come with me, Paige," he asked. "I could use the help."

She was tempted—so very tempted. But in the end, she knew better than to spend any more time with Christian than was absolutely necessary. Already, he'd managed to chip away at the walls she'd built up around her heart to protect herself from getting hurt again by a big star. She couldn't allow the walls to crumble any further. Not if she wanted her heart to remain in one intact piece when he left at the end of the week.

"I've got to take care of some work here," she said, "but have fun. And good work today."

She could see that he was disappointed that she wasn't going with him, but he didn't try to push her. Neither, she noted, did he rush out of the studio. Instead, he stared into her eyes long enough, and intensely enough, for her to wonder if he might be about to kiss her.

In the end, he simply said, "Thank you, Paige. I couldn't ask for a better dance teacher than you." Even though he hadn't given her the kiss that she could no longer deny she wanted, her heart was fluttering wildly in her chest as she watched him go.

CHAPTER SIX

Thanks to Christian's dash to a souvenir shop and the FedEx office, Paige got home much earlier than she had anticipated. She went straight upstairs, heading for the shower, hoping the hot water would help to wash away some of the day, too.

"Not touching him." Paige shook her head at the foolishness of that approach.

Now that she didn't have those piercing green eyes on her, it was easy to see just how silly she had been. Besides, what had she been doing, allowing herself to be unsettled by a man who was spending time with her only because he needed to learn to dance? How could she have wasted a whole day of practice when they needed every second of serious dancing time they could get?

Face to face, cheek to cheek, that was how they needed to be dancing together. But even as she thought it, a vision came of what it would be like to be held against his strong muscles, pressing close to him as they danced...

"Stop it," Paige told herself as she stepped out of the shower. While she had spent all day looking at Christian and thinking about how handsome he was, how wonderful, how sweet—she knew all he could have possibly seen when he looked back at her was nothing more than a dance instructor ready to put him through Fred Astaire boot camp over Christmas.

She'd been so busy trying to avoid looking like the cliché of the island girl falling for the big star that she'd become a paralyzed star-struck fan instead. Which was especially crazy considering she didn't even idolize Christian Greer. Until a couple of weeks ago, she hadn't really known much about him or his TV show. Well, not unless her father was over at the house and grabbed the remote to put on Christian's show, or when Grams felt like watching it. Not more than a few times a month, at most.

"So I should have absolutely no problem with touching him," Paige said to herself as she settled on a soft, flowing skirt and a royal blue sweater, leaving her hair down for once to let the soft waves bounce naturally.

Really, she thought now that she had the benefit of a little distance from it all, it wasn't like either of them was suddenly going to fall head over heels in love with the other. Fortunately, she had an entire night to pull herself together and get used to the idea of working closely with Christian on a purely professional basis.

When Paige went downstairs with a much clearer head than she'd come back from the studio with, she realized all the Christmas decorations were up. How could she not have noticed until right now? She had to laugh at herself, thinking of the time Michael had practically rebuilt the kitchen and she hadn't noticed for a week because her life had been such a blur between teaching at the dance studio, coming home to eat a quick meal, and then sleeping until it was time to get up and teach again. Thankfully, it was a beautiful blur Paige loved, filled with students who always managed to amaze her with their progress and joy in dance.

In any case, it was good to have Morgan back home and in charge of the decorations. With her flair for design, the house looked especially beautiful this Christmas. Paige could easily guess that her sister had hung the decorations with Charlotte in tow. Their niece had clearly wanted to put glitter everywhere, and of course Morgan had been only too happy to indulge the sweet little girl.

There were miles of tinsel, decorations on every available surface, lots of colorful and shiny baubles hanging from the ceiling, and so many assorted Santa Clauses that their home could have been the location of a holiday trade show.

At the center of it all was the tree. Paige smiled at the memory of Christmas trees from her childhood. They'd always been big and beautiful, filling the room. She and her sisters had worked together to decorate it while their mother, father, and grandmother cheered them on. Hanna had usually been the one wanting to add more ornaments to it. Morgan always liked to have a specific color theme. Rachel would volunteer to climb the ladder to put the angel at the top. And Emily would meticulously sort the presents into neat piles underneath.

The tree this year was everything she remembered. Big enough that it was a wonder they had managed to get it through the door. Brightly decorated to the point where it was almost hard to believe there was a tree under all of the ornaments and lights, with the angel placed on top.

The house was quiet for this time of day. She had expected Grams or Emily to be here somewhere, and given that everyone was on the island for the holidays, it was surprising that the rest of her sisters weren't filling up the house, too.

With all the decorations throughout the house, it took a little time before Paige noticed the note from Emily propped on the mantelpiece between a snow globe and a Santa Claus music box.

Grams and I have gone over to Seattle to do some Christmas shopping. Hanna and Rachel are at Dad's place. Charlotte is staying over at Morgan's. So the house is yours for the night. Have fun!

Momentarily, Paige was at a loss as to what to do for the evening. She thought about going over to see her father, Hanna, and Rachel. He lived only a short distance away, in the middle of town. It would be nice to visit with all of them—a nice end to a day that had been so frustrating.

On the other hand, she saw far more of her father than her other sisters did and knew it would be good to give him a chance to visit with them on their own. Besides, with Nicholas and Joel in tow, his small cottage would be full to bursting.

Suddenly, a light bulb went off in Paige's head. "I get to control the TV for once," she said with a smile. How often did she find herself alone in the house? As much as she loved her sister and grandmother, it was nice to have some space every now and again to watch whatever shows *she* wanted. Especially since the others tended to veto her collection of dance movies. Apparently, she and Grams were the only ones who loved watching the same movies for the hundredth time so that they could work through the dance sequences.

Another idea made Paige smile even wider: She was the only one in the family who liked to order takeout.

She went into the kitchen to look through the drawer where she kept a collection of takeaway menus from the local restaurants. What would it be tonight? Indian? Thai? Local seafood? Though

Walker Island was small, the number of tourists who visited meant it had a good selection of restaurants.

Inevitably, though, Paige settled on Chinese. She looked over the menu, working her way down through the selections to see what caught her eye. What hadn't she had in a while? She took the menu over to her collection of dance-inspired DVDs, planning to match the food with the video. *Flashdance* with ginger beef, maybe? *Strictly Ballroom* with kung pao chicken, perhaps?

Paige was still contemplating the perfect combination when the doorbell rang. It wouldn't be one of the family because they all had keys for the house. Could it be that Michael had decided to ring the doorbell, rather than just come in the way he normally did? He was a talented carpenter and builder, and there probably wasn't a single part of the house that he hadn't renovated, redecorated, or simply repaired. When he wasn't doing that, he was helping Grams with her laptop. Sometimes, if he was in the neighborhood, he would simply stop by to say hello. Emily was forever muttering about the way he *always* seemed to be here, but Paige thought Emily was pretty darn clueless if she hadn't figured out the real reason behind Michael's regular appearances. Especially since everyone else in their family could see that he'd been desperately in love with Emily ever since they were teenagers.

"Coming!"

She turned on the porch light and opened the door, shocked to find Christian rather than Michael on the front step. He looked so good in a checked shirt and slacks that it took her longer than it should have to realize that he had come bearing gifts. Namely, Chinese takeout in a bag from her favorite Chinese restaurant. Paige could also see he was holding a DVD, and a quick glance confirmed it was *Shall We Dance*.

He'd come over with takeout and a dance movie? On the one night when her family wasn't in? Had he read her mind? Was this all some kind of dream? Because having Christian, Chinese takeout, and her favorite movie all in one evening certainly sounded like a perfect fantasy.

"I ran into your sister and grandmother in town, and they said they were off to Seattle and that you were home on your own." Then he added, with a smile, "After today, I realize more than ever that I'm going to need to work not just harder, but smarter, too. So I've come up with a plan."

CHAPTER SEVEN

As Paige stepped back to let him in, Christian got his second view of the Walker house. It felt quiet and more intimate tonight with only Paige at home.

He noted that her cheeks were beautifully flushed as he explained, "When I saw your grandmother and she asked me how the dancing had progressed today, I couldn't lie to her. And then I asked both her and Emily if there was anything I could do to make it up to you—apart from trying harder tomorrow."

"What did they say?"

"Your grandmother said to relax and consider tomorrow a brand new start. And then Emily suggested I pick up some Chinese takeout and bring it over as a peace offering. She said you *love* Chinese takeaway." He grinned at her, pleased when she grinned back. "So, here I am with shrimp fried rice and sweet and sour chicken."

"Which one of them suggested the DVD?"

"That was actually *my* idea. After we have dinner, I hope we can watch the movie so that I can get a few pointers from you."

"You thought of everything, didn't you?"

With her hair down and curling softly around her face, and her eyes bright with pleasure at getting to eat her favorite food and watch one of her favorite movies, it took every ounce of his self-control not to give in to kissing her.

"I hope so," he said in a voice that held more emotion than he'd intended to reveal this quickly. The last thing he wanted to do was scare her away, so he followed that up with, "Will this work for you? Me coming over unannounced with food and a movie? Or would you rather spend the evening without me?"

"I'm glad you're here," Paige said without hesitation, and Christian breathed an inner sigh of relief. "Besides, how could I turn you down?" she asked, her eyes sparkling. "Chinese takeout is my favorite."

"In that case," he said, "how about we grab a couple of forks and eat directly out of the containers?"

"A man after my own heart," she agreed with a smile as she pulled out two forks and led the way to the family room, which now looked more like Santa's palace than a quiet sanctuary for adults.

"Did you do all of this?" Christian asked, looking around.

"No, my sisters and niece did. As you can see, we Walkers don't do things by halves."

"I'm glad to hear it. Because if today was anything to go by, I fully understand that you mean to kick my butt until I get this dance thing down. And, speaking of butts, I have to tell you that mine is killing me right now."

"You'll become a much better dancer than you were today," Paige promised him, laughing at his joke. Though he was serious, given that every muscle in his body was screaming. "I'll make *sure* that you do."

Christian knew she was serious, too. It had been intriguing to watch her work today and to see just how much her work meant to her. She was an excellent teacher, even if things had seemed a little strained between them at times during the day.

However, as much as he might want to pretend otherwise, his intentions for coming over tonight hadn't been entirely about the dancing. How could they be, when he found himself so drawn to Paige whenever they were in the same room? And when he couldn't take his eyes off of her?

Their day together had made the attraction he felt for her only stronger. The dance studio was where Paige seemed at her most natural and confident, her every movement graceful, smooth, and elegant. Sexy, too, whether she knew it or not. She hadn't even danced with him, but she'd been incredible all the same as she'd demonstrated how to perform each movement.

"Have a seat," Paige said, moving over to the DVD player.

He was gripped by the need to simply be near her, which wouldn't be easy if she picked a chair on the opposite corner of the room rather than the couch. On the other hand, he did have the food.

Christian almost laughed out loud at that thought. Here he was, a TV star and yet he was relying on a bag of Chinese takeout to ensure that he could get a seat close to Paige. Fortunately, his prayers were answered when Paige did sit beside him on the sofa, reaching out to help unpack the cartons of food.

They were both ravenous, and as they dug into the food, they talked easily. Paige's walls, it seemed, were starting to come down.

He couldn't have been more pleased.

When their conversation came around to Morgan's career, he said, "Your sister must have taken you around a few movie sets before now."

"Actually, Morgan was always off the island while she was doing makeup for movies, so we didn't ever get a chance to see any set—or her, either—for lots of years. Far too many years, actually."

"It's never easy, being away from your family for work, no matter how glamorous the work looks from the outside," he agreed. "I imagine it's tough on Brian when Morgan is away."

"Fortunately, she's able to shoot her

makeover show at the new studio on her property most of the time," Paige told him. She studied his face for a moment and added, "You must be missing your own family terribly this Christmas."

"I am missing them," he said, "but at the same time, I don't regret being here. I might not be with my own family, but it sure feels like I've landed in the middle of a really nice one."

"Grams and my sisters are always so welcoming," Paige agreed.

Didn't Paige see that *she* was the one who made his breath come quicker from just looking at her? Couldn't she see that *she* was the reason he would never regret coming here? Because if he hadn't, he would never have met her, and even after having known her such a short while, he already knew she was everything he could ever have hoped for in a woman: talented and beautiful, patient and clever.

Simply *amazing*.

Paige put her chopsticks down to pick up the remote and click the play button to start the movie. "What's your favorite scene?"

Christian found himself feeling more than a little embarrassed as he confessed, "Actually, I haven't seen the whole thing. I researched the history of the movie, of course, and I have watched some of the dance sections to get a feel for them. But I was hesitant to watch the whole thing because I was afraid that watching it might make me more inclined to outright copy Fred

Astaire's mannerisms and inflections rather than putting my own spin on the character."

Paige didn't respond straight away, and Christian had the feeling that rather than immediately judging him for not having yet watched, she was actually mulling over his reasons.

"Are you sure you'd like to watch it for the first time with me?" she finally asked.

Christian nodded. "I am."

"Even though you wanted to avoid seeing it before now?"

"There are some movies where, if I worked on the remake, it would probably make sense not to watch the film. But after working with you today, I've started to see that *Shall We Dance* probably isn't one of them. And what better time to watch it than with an expert like you?"

Her mouth curved up a tiny bit at the corners right before she said, "I wouldn't call myself an expert."

Of course she wouldn't. Paige was clearly the last person to ever sing her own praises. "How many times have you watched this movie?"

Paige paused before giving him the most beautiful smile he'd ever seen. One that actually stole his breath as she said, "Quite a few." Her smile grew even bigger as she amended that to, "A few dozen, actually."

"I expected the number to be big, but that is seriously impressive."

"I know it might sound crazy," she admitted

cheerfully, "but I'm always happy to watch it again." As the film began, she said, "The opening sequence doesn't often get a lot of attention, but this lift is just perfect."

With that, they settled deeper into the couch to watch the movie.

The styles of acting had changed a lot since *Shall We Dance* was filmed in the 1930s, and he could tell that Astaire had been brought up on stage rather than with a camera a few inches away capturing a close-up. The plot was pretty light, too, but was it any sillier than half the Hollywood blockbusters or romcoms being released? In fact, the deeper they got into the film, the more he realized just how delightfully whimsical and captivating the plot twists and turns were.

"This is such a good part," Paige said, breaking in with another bit of commentary as Astaire launched into a dance number in the engine room of the steamship, every movement seeming to coordinate with the movement of the pistons. Christian had seen fragments of the sequence before, but now that he understood the context around it, its sense of style and timing were even more impressive.

Doing a good job in this role mattered more than ever now. Not only because he always strove to do better and better with each project, but also because it mattered so much to Paige. Christian could see the rapt attention on her face as she watched the film closely—at least when she wasn't glancing over at him to see if he was taking it all in.

"It looks like there are many different types of dance going on in this," Christian ventured.

Paige's face lit up in a smile. "Well spotted. It was something Fred Astaire was trying to do at this stage of his career—blending tap, jazz, ballet. In fact, they had to bring in an extra ballet choreographer to help with that. These days, that blending is normal, but back then, it was something really special and unique."

Christian would have known just how special it was from the animated way Paige spoke about it. Throughout, she kept looking like she wanted to get up from the couch and dance along with the film.

He felt a nice kind of camaraderie being here with her, something he hadn't felt with another woman. It was as if the two of them were a unit, just them against...well, against all the dance steps that were to come, perhaps.

"Can I get you something to drink—a beer or a soda?" Paige asked.

"That would be great. Soy sauce always makes me thirsty."

She put the movie on pause and went into the kitchen to grab some drinks. When she came back, she had also brought in a tray of Christmas cookies. "Emily has been baking up a storm, and there are cookies and truffles and squares for days. *Somebody* has to eat all this stuff, and after all the calories you burned off today, a few wouldn't hurt."

When they settled back down on the sofa this time, they were sitting a little closer together. Close enough that he couldn't help but feel hyperaware of her—her breathing, her concentration, even just the simple fact that she was there with him.

Christian continued to watch the movie, with Paige providing a wonderful counterpoint to it, everything on the screen triggering some small reaction from her, whether it was drumming her fingers in time to the music or her tiny sounds of happiness as Fred Astaire delivered the key lines.

It felt so right to simply be curled up on the sofa with her enjoying a movie that she'd seen so many times she knew it by heart. Even more than that, it felt like *home*. Being here on Walker Island, in this big rambling old house with Paige Walker captivating him more and more with every moment that passed, was nothing less than perfect.

CHAPTER EIGHT

Dance practice went better the next day. *Much* better.

"You're doing a great job, Christian. Watching the movie must have really inspired you last night."

"The movie helped," he agreed, "but I just so happen to have a great teacher, too."

Now that they were actually dancing together, his posture had improved, his holds were so much better, and he could sustain them for much longer. She hardly had to remind him to change or fix anything today.

"For this next sequence, you'll need to stay as close to me as possible."

Christian looked down into her eyes and smiled. "I'll do my best."

When he smiled at her like that, it was hard not to get distracted and simply stare back at him like a love-struck girl. But every time her mind started to wander away from dancing, she reminded herself just how much there was for them to get through...and how little time they had.

Today, the plan was to work through a couple of sequences from the movie. It had been a leap of faith on her part that today would go better than yesterday had—well enough for them to actually be able to *dance*—but fortunately it had been the right decision. Even if they were soon both covered in sweat, breathing hard from the sheer effort of trying to do everything the dance required.

Something else was making it difficult, though: the two of them, pressed together, with Christian in his workout clothes and Paige in her leotard and tights. She had danced with many other partners, but it had never felt this intimate before. Not even, she was surprised to realize, with Patrice.

They worked alone in the studio until it almost seemed like the outside world didn't exist, pushing ahead even when they both were exhausted. They danced until Paige finally looked at her watch and saw that it was long past dinnertime.

"We've been working really, really hard. We should probably call it a day."

"Do you want to get something to eat?" Christian asked. "Takeout, maybe?"

If he hadn't added the word *takeout*, Paige might not have agreed to it. Because after spending the entire day staring into his eyes as they danced—and working like crazy to keep her heart from fluttering faster from every moment she spent in his strong arms—she would have been worried that a dinner out meant more than it really did.

Yet *takeout* was the magic word that meant they were still nothing more than teacher and student. Well, that wasn't exactly true. She felt that they were becoming friends.

And *friends* was—and would have to be—good enough for her.

* * *

They ended up back at her house again, this time with seafood and a copy of *Flying Down to Rio,* another Fred and Ginger movie from the 30s. Emily and Grams were home, but they were both too busy wrapping presents to do more than say hello.

"Fred Astaire and Ginger Rogers look so natural together," Christian said as they watched the two actors move effortlessly across the dance floor in the film. "It's as if they've been dancing together forever."

He was sitting next to her on the couch, as close as he'd been the night before—although it wasn't anywhere near as close as they'd been to one another all day. By now, she was surprised that it felt perfectly natural to have Christian so near.

"Actually, this was the first time they ever danced together on screen," Paige told him. "In fact, it's the first time Ginger Rogers *ever* danced with a partner."

"The first time?" Christian looked shocked. "Amazing."

It occurred to Paige that there was probably a lesson here she could use. "Fred Astaire said later that when they started out together, there were a lot of things Ginger couldn't do. She couldn't tap, for example."

"But she obviously worked twice as hard with her instructor and she got better?" Christian guessed, a really cute smile on his face as he said it.

Paige laughed. "I'm sure she did. Although what I'm trying to say is that while Ginger wasn't the most technical partner Fred Astaire ever worked with, she was able to make it look so perfectly natural when they danced together, because she could *act* her way through it. She was such a great actress that she could get across the intimacy between them despite the dancing skill she might have lacked. And that's why they ultimately ended up having such perfect chemistry together."

Christian watched Ginger and Fred dance on screen for a few more seconds before he turned back to Paige. "That's what I need to focus on when I dance, isn't it? More intimacy and all the emotions that come with it?"

The thought of becoming more intimate with him as they danced made a flush of heat rise around her face. "I'm going to do everything I can to give you technical dance skills, but the main thing you need to remember is that the acting doesn't stop just because the music has started. With dance, there's nowhere you can hide. You have to put everything you are into it. You have to throw in all your passion, all your energy. When you're dancing and you're in the zone, people quickly see what's there. You have the bonus of being able to take people through a range of emotions. Combine that with the skills I'm teaching you, and I think you'll be amazing in the movie."

* * *

The next day in the studio, Paige felt a new kind of intensity from him. One that felt deeply intimate and connected to her as his dance partner. They were working on one of the big numbers toward the end of the film that Christian really needed to acquire the skills for, and she decided to give almost the whole day over to it, stopping only when he started to drag.

Maybe his fatigue was part of his newfound intensity. Or maybe it was the sheer number of steps he needed to master. The choreographer on the movie would undoubtedly do plenty of work with him, and from what Paige understood, he was going to have a separate tap instructor. Yet there were still so many dance sequences in the original movie, and there was no reason to believe that any of them would be excluded in the remake.

Whatever it was, by the middle of the afternoon, his fatigue was hard to ignore. Truthfully, she was feeling it herself. Although she taught every day, there was a big difference between standing in front of a class giving instructions and demonstrations and working closely with someone as a dance partner. If they'd had the time, she might have called a halt for the day, but they couldn't afford to lose any more time. And she was more than a little concerned that he still wasn't leading the way he should.

She'd been playing around with an idea in her head all day, one that took only a quick phone call during their water break to solidify.

"Come on," she told him. "We're going on a field trip."

"A field trip? Where are you taking me?"

"I was hoping you would take us, actually," she told him with a smile. "Our destination isn't far, but I thought it might be nice to get off our feet for a few minutes, if you wouldn't mind driving."

She directed him to the location she had in mind, enjoying the look on Christian's face once he saw the sign next to the parking lot she asked him to turn into.

"You're taking me to a roller-skating rink?"

"Where else are we going to practice the parts for *Let's Call the Whole Thing Off*?" She gave him a mischievous smile. "The owners have gone to Seattle for the holidays, but their daughter said she would unlock it for me."

They went inside, and Karen was there to help them pick out some roller skates, the other woman's jaw dropping when she realized who Christian was. He instantly smiled, putting Karen at ease and even agreeing to let her take a selfie with him.

"Thanks so much. Paige, when you're done, can you lock up here? I need to get home."

After Karen left, Paige looked back at Christian and said, "She clearly couldn't wait to tell everyone about this. I suspect the news that you're here skating is probably going to be all around the island by the time we're done."

Christian just laughed. He didn't seem to mind. "What matters is that we're here and ready to dance."

That was probably a little overly optimistic. At first, they were barely able to stand up. Christian slipped as they moved out onto the rink, at which point Paige promptly fell on top of him as her feet skidded out from under her, too. Christian felt so solid—and so good—beneath her, that she tried to scramble back to her feet again to put at least a tiny bit of space between them so that she could get her breath back. Of course, she managed only to fall right back down again.

After a few minutes, thankfully, they both managed to get to their feet and stay there! Paige had spent her life dancing, but clearly, dancing and roller-skating were two very different things. Her feet seemed to have minds of their own, wanting to go in every direction but the ones she actually wanted them to go in. She started to fall over again, grabbing for the side wall in desperation.

Christian seemed to be having the same problems, but that didn't stop him from having a good laugh over their clumsiness. It was fun, she realized, watching him being out of control but perfectly happy about it—and letting herself feel the same way as laughter bubbled up and out of her, too.

"Maybe skating wasn't such a great idea," Paige said as she took another step and nearly skidded off her feet again. "I thought it would be a nice way to get out of the studio for a while and work on our balance, but..." She laughed. "Now I just think we should get out of these skates before we hurt ourselves!"

She went to sit down on the wooden benches and slipped her feet out of the skates. Christian soon sat beside her and did the same.

Except, once their skates were off, she looked up and realized that Christian was standing in front of her, holding out his hand. There was a twinkle in his eye and a sense of grace to the movement, despite the fact that he was standing there in his socks.

In that moment, he *was* Fred Astaire...and Paige couldn't wait to be his Ginger Rogers.

She held out her hand and Christian took it smoothly, taking her into the moves they'd been practicing earlier. He was leading her perfectly this time, sweeping Paige up in the whirl of the movement.

She felt as if they could have been in a black-and-white movie just then. There was no music, but he had the steps memorized, and the timing of them seemed to come from somewhere inside him. She flowed with him around the skating rink as though it was the perfect dance floor, until he finally spun her into the last movement of the dance.

"You did it!" Paige said breathlessly. "*You actually did it!*"

Christian seemed every bit as ecstatic as she was. He held her tightly in his arms for a moment or two, looking deep into her eyes as the moment was suspended in time, as if there was no place he'd rather be and no one else he'd rather be with.

And then he kissed her.

CHAPTER NINE

Christian led their kiss as effortlessly as he had led the dance, his lips pressing against Paige's with the mix of joy and desire. Paige kissed him back with just as much passion, because in that moment it felt *exactly* like the right thing to do. And even though they'd been close while they'd been dancing, their sweetly seductive kiss felt so much more intimate.

She'd always dreamed of a kiss like this. A kiss just like the ones in the movies—sweet and passionate, tender and powerful, all at once.

Christian drank in her smile, saying, "I love seeing you look so happy."

"I am. I really am."

He drew her close again and held her, his cheek against the top of her head. Their kiss had been so perfect, so unexpected, but at the same time such a natural continuation of everything that had been happening over the last couple of days. It had been so easy to get caught up in the excitement of their dance...and so worth it when she had.

He had been in the zone from the moment that he'd held out his hand to her. Of course, there was still so much for him to learn as a dancer, but the Fred Astaire feeling that they were going for had definitely been there. While they'd danced, she had been able to feel his intensity of emotion and the way he had led every step. With his acting skills, he had made their dance far more than just a set of choreographed movements: He had made it *beautiful*.

"You were perfect, Christian."

"So were you."

She had been talking about his dancing—at least she thought she was, wasn't she?—but

was he? Or was he talking about their kiss? One she knew she'd replay over and over in her head for a very long time to come.

Still, she was on too much of a high to worry about any of that right now. "You can really do this. You can pull this movie off! I'm sure of it now." When he had first arrived, the truth was that she hadn't actually thought he'd get to the stage where he could be convincing in one of Astaire's dances. And then when she'd first seen him try to dance, she'd been sure that her teaching skills would not be up to the task. But now, after experiencing the wonder of one perfect dance with him in the middle of the empty roller-skating rink, she knew better.

He moved to take her hands as they stood near the entrance to the rink. "You really think so?"

Paige had heard a note of nervousness in his voice only a handful of times. Once had been on the first day, when he'd been down on the floor doubting himself, and then a couple of times after that, when the moves had been really challenging. Yet, now she was surprised to see that her approval meant so much to him.

"Absolutely, yes! If you can dance like that all the time, you're going to be great. That was the first time I really *felt* something while you danced, way deep down the way I've needed to feel it."

Something beyond the fundamental attraction of being close to him, at least. Paige had felt *that* from the start, of course. Most women would, she knew. But what she'd felt when they'd been dancing just now had been so much more than that. Something had changed. Something had shifted. In the best possible way.

"What you said last night about Ginger Rogers acting her way through it made a huge difference," he told her. "If you hadn't been here with me every step of the way, if you hadn't known how to put things in exactly the right way, so that I could think like a dancer, I would never have known *how* to dance like that."

Hearing his praise, Paige felt a wave of satisfaction run through her. She was always happy when one of her students had a breakthrough, but with Christian it felt like so much more. Just seeing him look so happy about his achievements was something so simple yet powerful. She could feel that happiness practically radiating from him.

She was also aware of how special he had made her feel, too. Here at the roller rink, it had felt like he'd transported her to another world where it was just the two of them. Where everything was amazing, and doing something crazy like kissing him was the most wonderful thing she'd ever experienced in her life.

Right then, she didn't feel even a hint of regret about the kiss they'd shared. How could she when it had been the perfect way to end a perfect dance?

"How about Indian takeout tonight?" Christian suggested as they gathered up the skates they'd taken off and put them away.

Paige loved the image of the two of them together on the couch once again. They'd been there the last couple of nights, but in the wake of their kiss, the image felt different. Tonight, it seemed to hold all kinds of promises. Promises that made Paige shiver slightly in anticipation, because being close to him now would never be the same. Even dancing with him held a different kind of anticipation now that they'd kissed.

"I'd love that," she said. "We'll have to find another great Fred Astaire movie to watch."

"Something tells me I haven't even begun to make a dent in your dance movie collection."

He was right. They still had plenty of movies to go through—and plenty of nights' worth of takeout. Paige could so easily imagine sharing her couch with Christian for many nights to come. She knew it was a dream, but right then it felt so good she wanted to believe that it could be true. His dancing had helped to transport her to a beautiful, magical world that she didn't want to leave. Not yet.

When he reached out to take her hand as they walked back to the car, she not only let herself enjoy being with him, she also allowed herself to look forward to more of his kisses once they got back to her place.

"There he is!" a voice shouted from the parking lot.

"Christian! Look this way!" someone else called.

A crowd of people were approaching them, phone cameras flashing. There were only a dozen or so people, but they were making enough noise for two or three times that many. Most of them appeared to be young women.

Paige immediately slipped her hand from Christian's, hoping no one had gotten a clear picture of them together.

"Karen must have posted something on the Internet," Paige said. How could she have forgotten that was going to happen? How could she have gotten so wrapped up in Christian that she'd forgotten about the real world?

He shrugged, as if it was the most natural

thing in the world for a crowd to be waiting outside for him. "Don't worry, I've got this. It wouldn't be right to just ignore them, but we won't be delayed long. I promise."

He turned on his full movie star smile as the crowd of fans got closer, moving forward slightly to meet them. "You must have been waiting for a while," he said to them, turning on the charm that came so effortlessly to him.

That was all it took for everyone to start talking at once, asking for autographs and photographs and wanting to discuss every detail of the current season of *Seattle General Medical*. In a matter of seconds, a cluster of women in their teens and early twenties literally surrounded Christian, all looking for attention from their favorite star.

They all got it, too. Every one of them. Christian stood at the center of the group, every inch the gracious star. Paige had thought her sister Morgan had star quality, but Christian's was at a whole other level, and as effortless as if he'd been born with it.

"I'm glad you're enjoying the show, Julia," he said, having apparently learned the names of everyone in the group in a matter of seconds. He spoke to one woman after another, and she could see that he made each feel as if she was the center of his world.

Paige remembered the way he'd been with her family when he arrived for dinner. He'd spoken to each member, making them feel as if he truly was interested in them and their stories. In a matter of minutes, he'd become a part of all their lives, making them feel like close friends.

Exactly like he did with me.

Just minutes ago, she'd been feeling so special, as if she and Christian understood one another perfectly—the Astaire to her Rogers. Just the two of them in their own little world, as if they'd meant something to each other.

Yet, here he was tonight outside the skating rink, doing what movie stars were meant to do by freely giving his time and attention to his loyal fans. And Paige knew that each of them probably felt as if *she* was the only woman in the world who mattered to him. As if there was some kind of special connection between them, and that if *only* they could have a little more time together, it might blossom into something special.

Paige's ex had a knack for making everyone around him feel special, too. At least when he wanted to. When Patrice was with someone he wanted to impress, or with a beautiful woman, he always managed to make them feel as if they were the most important thing in his life. He'd certainly made Paige feel that way.

But the truth was that Patrice was the most important thing in Patrice's life. The rest of the world had been nothing more than a cast of extras caught up in the grand story of his life, with Paige meaning little more to him than a walk-on part. A minor love interest to be enjoyed and discarded with no more thought than you'd give a side character in a ballet once the performance was over. She had only momentarily been the center of his world until he had the choreography he wanted, and then she hadn't been of any importance to him at all.

Of course, Paige knew Christian wasn't just using her to get what he wanted the way Patrice had—she had willingly agreed to be his dance instructor. And Christian also didn't have an ounce of disdain for his fans. He was giving his all to them because he was a wonderful, generous man.

At the same time, if she was really honest with herself, she should have known better than to read too much into his kiss at the end of their one perfect dance. It wasn't Christian's fault that she had. It was her fault for thinking that one kiss—even one *amazing* kiss—would mean more than it really had. He was here to learn how to dance for a movie, and after the week was over, he would be gone. But she would still be here, nursing yet another broken heart, unless she was a whole lot more careful to guard it around him than she'd been so far.

As Christian's fans asked him to pose for more pictures and sign more autographs, Paige slipped quietly away from the crowd.

CHAPTER TEN

Even as the fans had clamored for Christian's attention, he'd been aware of Paige the whole time and saw her begin to slip away. He was about to call out her name to ask her to wait a couple more minutes, when one of the young women in the crowd put a hand on his arm.

"Christian, it would make my *entire* day if we could take a photo together! I totally loved the last season of *Seattle General Medical.* I swear I'm your biggest fan."

He always found it amazing just how committed fans could be to actors they had only seen on a screen. Which was, of course, why he did his best to live up to their expectations when he met them. Without fans like them, he wouldn't have a career, and that's why he always felt that he owed them at least a little attention.

"Why have you come to Walker Island?" the woman asked as her friend took their picture.

"Have you decided that you want to live here?"

He could hear the breathless excitement in her question. He could feel it from practically the whole group, actually. It was exactly the kind of excited question that could start a rumor.

"I'm sorry to disappoint you, but I'm here to do research for a role." He wasn't sure that saying he was here to learn to dance would be a good idea. People might work out that there was only one place on the island where he could do that, and then he and Paige might find themselves with an audience for their dance sessions.

Paige. Just thinking of her made his heart do a flip in his chest. Their dance had been amazing. But their kiss had been extraordinary. He'd felt as if they were finally getting a chance to explore the connection between them that had been there since Christian arrived on the island, and he couldn't have been happier about it.

Wanting to continue deepening their connection where they'd left off, he was just about to let his fans know he had to leave when one of the other young women asked, "What's it like when you have to kiss one of your co-stars? I mean, I know you don't really have a relationship, but you're still kissing them, aren't you?"

"You've answered your own question," he said with a smile. "It's not real."

"But it looks so real on-screen!"

Even if he had only just met the actress he was kissing on-screen, he was good at convincing the audience that whatever their characters felt for one another was the truth, running far deeper than the story currently being told. "Then I suppose we're doing a good job as actors, aren't we?" Christian's laugh turned that into a joke for everyone. But it was no joke how so many of the rumor mills had him linked with most of his co-stars. Being able to portray a connection with someone like that was a double-edged sword.

And it was *nothing* like what he was experiencing with Paige.

For once in his life Christian had an emotional connection to a woman that was everything his romantic acting roles promised. Only, with Paige, there was no pretending. No layers of character providing the emotion. No cameras.

Instead, it was just the two of them, a woman and a man falling for each other in the most natural, and honest, way possible as they danced in each other's arms.

"I hope you all enjoy the rest of your evening," Christian said as he finished signing his last autograph in a hurry, looking around for Paige. It was only as he pried himself free from the crowd of admirers that he finally realized she had disappeared.

He knew big groups of fans could be overwhelming for some people. And after the comments she'd made at dinner that first night about not understanding how anyone could enjoy being famous, it wasn't difficult to guess that his group of enthusiastic fans had probably pushed at the edges of her comfort zone.

But was that the only reason she'd gone? Or was there another reason that she'd run?

Could she have decided she regretted their kiss, after all?

He got back in his car, knowing immediately where she would have gone to seek refuge. Not the family house, regardless of how much she loved her sisters and grandmother. No, for Paige, there would be only one place that would truly soothe her if she felt off-kilter.

The dance studio.

When he pulled up outside the studio, he could see that the lights were on. The door was unlocked, so he went in, wanting to talk to her. Wanting to ask her why she'd left. Wanting to kiss her again. Wanting to see her beautiful smile as they danced together.

The sight of Paige alone in the middle of the dance floor was enough to make Christian's breath catch. She was in the same clothes she'd worn to the skating rink, but her hair was down, falling loose past her shoulders in a golden wave as she danced to the song *They All Laughed* from *Shall We Dance*. He knew from watching the movie with her that it was Fred Astaire's part she was dancing, rather than Ginger Rogers' supporting role.

How was it possible, he found himself wondering as he watched her move gracefully across the floor, to dance with someone for a couple of days and never see them truly dance?

But he already knew the answer—Paige had been concentrating on teaching him, not showing off her own abilities. Even when they danced together, she rarely concentrated on herself.

Now, it was easy to see how much she'd held back just to let him keep up. She moved so gracefully, so perfectly, so effortlessly, giving herself up to the music completely.

Because Paige had talked him through most of the choreography in this dance, Christian could remember the general shape of it. Enough to realize that this wasn't the original. That more expansive leap hadn't been in there, because Christian was sure he would have remembered it. And several other moves looked like they owed more to street dance than to Fred Astaire. Even the parts he did remember had their own little beautiful twists.

Through it all, there was an amazing intensity to her dancing—a sweet and pure joy that spilled over into the room. When Paige got to her version of the tap duet at the heart of the piece, Christian found his own feet tapping softly on the floor outside, trying to keep up. He was so swept up in the moment, and in her, that it was impossible to remain still.

More than anything, he wanted step in there and join her. He wanted to take her in his arms and finish the dance with her pressed close to him. He wanted her to look at him the way she had back at the skating rink. And he wanted both of them to get lost in another kiss.

But as he watched her dance more beautifully than anyone else ever had, he knew that this moment wasn't meant for him. Paige wasn't putting on a show. She was dancing for the joy of dancing, just her and the music. As much as he wanted to deepen his connection with her, this was her own private moment. One she'd clearly needed after everything that had happened with them at the rink.

If anyone understood privacy, it was him. He knew what it was like to stand in the middle of a crowd and wonder if your life was your own. Paige obviously wanted this moment for herself, without him, or anyone else, interfering. And regardless of how badly he wanted to be with her, he couldn't bear to take the moment away from her.

Knowing that he had to leave and yet wanting to see her dance for just a few seconds more, Christian finally forced himself to turn and shut the door carefully behind him.

CHAPTER ELEVEN

Christian arrived at the dance studio earlier than usual the next morning, hoping Paige would also be there so that they would have time to talk before they got back into dance training. Christmas Eve, and yet here he was, ready to dance. Ready to train. Eager for it even. But so much more eager to see Paige, who looked positively gorgeous this morning, in close-fitting dance pants and a crop top that revealed an inch or so of toned skin.

But when she saw him and he opened his mouth, he realized that he wasn't sure what to say—or how to say it. Not when he had a feeling that getting it just right was crucially important right now, especially given the wary look in Paige's eyes.

"Yesterday...at the rink..."

"You danced really, really well," she cut in. "And now that we know exactly what you're capable of, we've *really* got to get cracking so that you can blow your director and co-star away when you show up on set in January."

He knew he still had a great deal to learn, but that didn't mean they needed to ignore the kiss they'd shared, did it?

Last night, after he'd left her to dance alone in the studio, he'd felt bereft without their usual takeout and movie. Because even though they'd done the movie and takeout thing only a couple of times, it had felt perfectly natural. Missing out on spending the evening with Paige had made him feel like something had gone terribly wrong.

"Paige, I think we need to talk."

Her eyes flashed, and for a moment, he thought she might tell him why she'd left him alone with the crowd of fans. But in the end, she quietly said, "I really think we should dance first."

Taking that as a promise that she wouldn't run from him again, even if it was abundantly clear that she wasn't looking forward to talking about what had happened yesterday, he nodded and they got to work. Dancing was what he was here for, after all, the whole point of this trip to Walker Island. Yet this morning, it felt utterly secondary to him. He couldn't help but think that their kiss—and the reasons Paige had left so suddenly afterward—should take center stage, not the dancing.

Especially not *this* dancing.

He was working to shut out everything but the music and his own body moving through space as, step by step, he tried to get his technique up to par. Paige, meanwhile, was a model of technical excellence, every step in time, every angle perfect.

So then why did it feel like they were so completely out of tune with one another?

They'd never been more technically in step together, but it felt like any connection they'd had was gone, buried under a flurry of movements and turns that didn't matter even half as much. Christian had seen this happen before on set, the kind of anti-chemistry that could ruin a day's shooting, taking lines that should have been full of life and communication and sucking all of the life from them.

"Paige." When Christian abruptly stopped dancing, Paige wasn't able to finish the spin she was halfway through. "Please, tell me what's wrong."

"Nothing is wrong," she replied, but the flatness of her voice didn't at all match her words. "You're hitting the turns and taking the lead in the holds. Your posture is improving, and your footwork is nearly perfect, too."

It was obvious that she was trying to dodge the issue, dancing around it as effortlessly as she danced around everything else. She wanted him to leave this alone, yet if he did, where did that leave them? What would it mean about everything that had been building up between them?

No, he wouldn't risk losing that, not even

after just a couple of nights.

"I looked for you last night, after you left the rink when the fans were there. I drove back to the studio."

Her eyes widened. "You did?"

"I didn't want to interrupt when I saw you dancing. You looked like you wanted to be alone." When she didn't say anything and he knew pushing her would only put a bigger distance between them, he decided to shift gears. "Where did you get that great new choreography for *They All Laughed*?"

"I was just messing around," she said modestly, "seeing what else I could do with it. It's not important."

"It was good. Really good." It hadn't just been the mesmerizing sight of Paige performing, although that had probably been a big part of it. It had been the beauty of the way she had blended so many unique elements to create something new. At her slightly doubtful look, he added, "I don't have to be the world's greatest dancer to know great choreography and amazing dancing when I see it."

Finally, she smiled at him. It wasn't a big smile, but it was *something*.

"You should show that sequence to the choreographer on the movie," Christian suggested. "You told me yourself that this movie was all about blending styles, so I'd bet that's just the kind of thing they're looking for."

He'd hoped he was managing to break

through the tension between them, but unfortunately, what he'd just said made her smile vanish as quickly as it had come. "I'm sure the choreographer they've hired already has things well in hand. Plus, your co-star Liana is a world-class dancer and will likely have some suggestions of her own to add. Whereas I'm just a dance teacher on a small island."

Her voice caught slightly on the word *island*, and Christian reached out for her, unable to stop himself. He wanted to comfort her. Wanted to make everything better. But though Paige didn't step back, she didn't reach out for him, either. And that hurt. A lot.

"Are you upset with me because we kissed?" He couldn't think what else it could be. What else had changed between them since yesterday? In the moments right after they'd kissed, he'd been so certain that it had brought them closer. It had been so wonderful that he had never thought about the possibility that it might drive them apart. But then she'd left without even saying good night.

"It's not the kiss," she said quickly.

But he could see that it was. "You have to know that I've been drawn to you from the first moment I met you, Paige. I just couldn't help but kiss you last night, even though I knew it was too soon."

"Too soon?" She looked absolutely shocked by what he'd just said. "Our kiss shouldn't have happened at all. We both just got caught up in the moment because we were excited with how well you were dancing." She swallowed hard and looked away. "We both know it didn't mean anything."

"That's not true," Christian said as he gently placed his hand beneath her chin to tip her face up to his so that he could look into her eyes. "It *was* something. We both know that it was. That it *is* something."

"Why don't I hear music?" Ava's voice cut through the thick tension in the dance studio. "Is Paige not working you hard enough, Christian? You should be dancing, not standing around talking."

Ava looked as spry and vivacious as ever as she walked in, but as soon as she looked from Christian to Paige and back, her eyebrows went up. "Ah, I can see that I'm interrupting. I'll just go—"

"No, Grams, don't go. Please."

Paige actually grabbed her grandmother's arm to stop her. Was she that desperate to keep from having the rest of this conversation with him? The last thing Christian wanted was to hurt her, but he didn't want to let go of the chance of a relationship with her, either. Not with the incredible connection that he'd felt between them.

And not when he couldn't stop remembering how happy Paige had seemed in the moments right before—and after—they'd kissed.

"Will you dance with Christian for me,

Grams?"

"So you're not going to be my partner anymore?" Christian tried to keep his question to Paige light, but he couldn't keep a note of frustration from creeping into his voice.

"I'd like to see how you dance with a partner you don't know," Paige replied, but even to Christian, it didn't sound like the whole truth.

Nonetheless, he walked over to Ava and held out a hand. She gracefully took it as Paige started the music, and together, he and Ava danced through the steps of the piece he and Paige had been working on. That Ava knew them was no surprise, given that she had been a dancer all her life, and he suspected Ava had been right there beside Paige on the couch watching the Fred Astaire movies again and again throughout the years.

"He's getting really good," Ava called out to Paige as they drifted smoothly around the floor. He did his best to add a touch of sweetness and humor to their dance that Ava mirrored effortlessly.

With Paige, though, he knew the dance would have been something very different: a courtship rather than a playful comedy. And he could feel Paige's eyes on him as he danced, following every movement he made. It could have just been his dance teacher wanting to make sure he did everything correctly, but he knew deep in his heart that it was more than that.

Far more, whether she wanted to admit that

to herself or not.

Finally, the music came to an end, and Ava laughed delightedly. "You've made me feel young again, Christian. It was like dancing with Fred all over again."

"Fred?" His mind boggled for a moment. "You danced with Fred Astaire?"

"You never told me that, Grams!" Paige sounded shocked that her grandmother hadn't already told her something like that.

Ava smiled at both of them, a smile that clearly held wonderful memories. "I've been a dancer for a long time, and I danced with plenty of great leading men. I might have even been lucky enough to be hanging around the set of *Let's Dance* at just the right moment."

Christian laughed at that. He could just imagine Ava managing to find her way onto the set of a movie where she had no business being. And dancing with Fred Astaire. Probably beautifully. Almost as beautifully as her granddaughter had danced. It was impossible not to like Ava, with her easy charm and liveliness.

"Fred was the lucky one getting to dance with you, Ava."

"You're very sweet, Christian," she said, and he knew that she was assessing him on her granddaughter's behalf. More than anything, he wanted her to think that he was good enough for Paige...and to know that her granddaughter's happiness was becoming the most important thing in the world to him.

Because while it had been wonderful to dance with Ava, the truth was that her visit had come at the worst possible moment, when there was still so much he needed to say to Paige.

"I'm sorry to have interrupted your practice session," Ava said, breaking into his thoughts, "but I didn't come down here just to dance, I'm afraid. I just got a call from the Walker Island Commission." Turning to him, she explained, "Every year we have a big tree-lighting ceremony at our Christmas Eve party."

He had a feeling he knew where the conversation was going, and it seemed Paige did, too, as she said, "They want Christian to light the tree, don't they? They've just assumed that because someone famous is here, of course he should agree to it."

Ava nodded, smiling apologetically at Christian. "I told them that I would ask you, mostly because I'd never hear the end of it if I didn't. Please feel free to say no. I know how busy you are right now, and it's unreasonable for the commission to ask on the night of the event like this." She made a disapproving sound.

"Are you going to be there?" Christian asked Paige.

"We all go over to the tree lighting. It's a family tradition."

"Then of course I'll do it," Christian said, holding her beautiful blue eyes with his and hoping she could see that he would have agreed to absolutely anything if it meant getting to be with her. "It sounds like fun."

CHAPTER TWELVE

The tree-lighting ceremony on Christmas Eve, held near the harbor, was a big deal on the island. It had started out as nothing more than the community's attempt to add a bit of festive cheer by gathering the locals to light up the most iconic area of their town. By now, though, it had become an event that practically everyone on the island attended, complete with music, entertainers, marine biologists who were staying for the holidays, great food and much more.

The *much more* included Paige and her sisters, who were all currently standing in a tent just off the main street while Morgan worked to finish their hair, wardrobe, and makeup with all the care and seriousness that she would have applied to big movie stars.

Movie stars like Christian, Paige thought, and then worked to squash that thought. Just like she'd tried to push away all the other thoughts she'd had of him that day. Not that it had worked, of course, when they'd spent the morning dancing together, as usual. And not that it *could* work when he was just so gorgeous and sweet all the time.

There she went again, when she knew as well as anyone that things couldn't possibly work between them. Because however much it was impossible to ignore their attraction when they were dancing in each other's arms, he was still a major movie star, and she was just a dance instructor on a small island. One who had made the big mistake of trying to date a star once before.

When Paige sighed as Morgan applied another flick of eye shadow and then a touch of lipstick, her sister gave her a reassuring smile. "One day, you'll be used to being the center of attention with all of us one night a year. Might take you a few decades, but you'll get used to it."

Morgan might have gotten used to it after all her time spent on TV, but Paige knew she never would. She looked around for something to distract her from the thought of walking out in front of so many people in a few minutes—and from constantly thinking about Christian. Her sisters all looked so beautiful in the red-and-white dresses they'd worn to fit with the seasonal theme. They each had the same dress, but they all managed to make it look so different.

Emily, for example, managed to look rather formal and elegant. Morgan looked as if she was about to attend a film premiere. Rachel looked fit and athletic from her traveling adventures with Nicholas and little Charlotte. Hanna, of course, had customized her dress into something far less formal and was carrying a small video camera to document the whole occasion. Then there was Paige, hoping she would be able to find a spot in the crowd where she could disappear into the background.

Still, it was hard to deny the sense of excitement bubbling up in her. Even if this event involved far too many people looking at her, the ceremony was one of the most beautiful moments of the year. She wondered what Christian would think about it.

Christian again. She worked to shake him out of her head as she turned to Rachel, ignoring Morgan's attempt to get her to stay still so that she could finish making her up.

"What's one of your favorite things you have done with Nicholas since you've been gone?"

"When we went to Japan, we went all the way up Mount Fuji. The view from the top was incredible." Rachel looked especially beautiful when she talked about the man she loved. "Although the view we got while we were hang-gliding in Chile was pretty darn spectacular, too."

Paige still couldn't believe the change in her sister from insurance actuary to a one-woman adventure daredevil. Actually, not one-woman, because she had Nicholas and Charlotte beside her all the way. Maybe that was why it worked so well for them. Or maybe it was just that this adventurous part of Rachel had been trying to get out for so long. Nicholas had been the one who had finally helped her sister to be who she really wanted to be. He was the loving partner in adventure she'd always wanted, and as far as Paige could see, he was a great father figure for Charlotte as well.

"You're not the only one who's been having adventures," Hanna said. "Joel has been teaching me how to sail."

The Walker and Peterson family feud had gone on for generations, but just a short while ago, Hanna and Joel had put an end to that. Their marriage would have been almost unthinkable a few years ago, yet now it was impossible to imagine Hanna and Joel apart.

"Once I've graduated from the university, we're talking about setting off on a round-the-world trip in his sailboat. I could turn the whole thing into a documentary about what makes people take on endurance sailing challenges and why sailing still means something in the modern world."

Paige loved listening to her sisters talk about their passions. "You have so many great ideas, Hanna. It's just wonderful."

Paige had had plenty of ideas, too, when she was younger. When she'd gone off to Juilliard, it had felt like her brain was overflowing with dance steps trying to get out. She'd been so confident that, in time, she would end up as a choreographer for a major dance company. Yet now that dream seemed as far away as the younger versions of Hanna and Rachel.

"Please," Morgan begged, "can you sit still? The one opportunity I get to give you a proper makeover each year, and you're squirming like Charlotte in the chair. If this takes any longer, Brian will probably be thinking that the rest of you have kidnapped me and dragged me off on one of your adventures."

"He'd only come looking for you if we did," Rachel pointed out. "The two of you look exactly the same together as you did in school—still all gooey-eyed when you look at each other."

Morgan didn't disagree, although she did laugh and say, "I'd like to think I've grown up a bit since then."

"You might like to think it," Hanna teased.

Paige sat back in her chair the way Morgan wanted her to and let herself enjoy being with all of her sisters. There weren't many moments like these anymore now that they all had their own lives. But that didn't mean they cared any less, and it certainly didn't mean they were about to stop teasing one another when they did get the chance.

"Rachel, Hanna, Morgan, you're all so lucky," Emily said with a small sigh. "I can't wait until I find a guy who loves me as much as yours love you."

That brought the conversation to a crashing halt for a few moments while everyone stared at her, open-mouthed. It wasn't that Emily had said anything wrong. In fact, Paige thought it was quite a sweet sentiment. It was just...couldn't she see what was right under her nose? Was she seriously saying that she'd never noticed just how much Michael *adored* her, especially when it was so obvious to the rest of them?

Paige thought briefly about speaking up. After all, if Emily was really that eager to find Mr. Right, then maybe she deserved that push in the right direction. But before she could, Emily asked her, "How are the dance lessons going with Christian?"

"They're going fine."

Emily raised an eyebrow. "You don't sound all that certain about it."

"It's just that things are..." She shook her head, not quite sure how to finish her sentence.

But when she looked back, Emily was smiling. "I know that look. I've seen it enough on the others in the past few months."

"What look?"

"Rachel, Hanna, you can see it, too, can't you?" Emily was obviously enjoying herself now. "The way Paige looks whenever someone mentions Christian Greer?"

Paige could feel her cheeks burning as her sisters looked at her.

"Well, it's pretty obvious that she likes him," Hanna agreed.

"You've been dancing cheek to cheek with him for days," Emily said. "And we all saw the way he couldn't take his eyes off of you when he was over for dinner. Seems to me that there's a lot more than just *liking* between you two. Isn't there, Paige?"

Was there any point in denying it? In trying to deny something that was so obvious even to Emily, who couldn't see what was right in front of her?

Paige stood up, ignoring Morgan's protest that she was going to smear her newly applied mascara if she wasn't careful. "So what if I maybe, possibly, have a tiny little crush on him? He's a gorgeous star. Do you know how many other women around the world have crushes on him?"

Although thinking about that wasn't a pleasant thought, either. She knew she could never have him and that she wasn't made for the world of movie stars and glamor, but that didn't mean she had to be happy about the thought of thousands of other women lusting over him.

"It isn't like my little crush matters. He's Christian Greer and I'm just me."

She was surprised when Morgan smiled after she said that. "I think maybe you should take a look in a mirror, Paige."

"You're done?"

Morgan turned her to look in one of the mirrors dotted around the tent, and for a moment Paige just stared, trying to recognize the person she saw in the reflection—a version of herself that Paige had never seen before. Morgan had taken the raw material of her features and used her makeup brush to craft something simply astonishing.

Morgan really was Michelangelo when it came to makeup. If she could do that much with Paige, then she had to be some kind of genius. Didn't she? Paige had never believed that she could look like this. Maybe she'd never wanted to. And now...

"Let's go everyone," Morgan said. "Everyone out there has been waiting for us long enough."

Paige walked out with the rest of her sisters. Actually, she strode out, feeling more confident than ever before. There was something about being all glammed up for the night that made it seem easy to step out in front of everyone with a smile on her face when before she would have been trying to hold back.

Everyone was staring at her and her sisters as they walked toward the low stage where Christian waited, obviously ready to flip the switch on the Christmas lights. He looked as amazing as always. Every inch the movie star.

Yet as she walked up onto the stage, he wasn't looking out at the crowd, charming everyone in the audience in that easy way he had with his fans. Instead, he was staring directly at her in a way that warmed Paige straight through, even in the chilly night air.

As she and her sisters lined up next to him, ready for their part in the big Christmas Eve ceremony, Emily whispered to him, just loud enough for Paige to hear, "Doesn't Paige look beautiful tonight?"

"Paige always looks beautiful," he said, his expression full of such sweet emotion that it took her breath away. "Always."

CHAPTER THIRTEEN

Christian stepped to the front of the stage, looking out over the crowd as he prepared to open the ceremony, working hard to concentrate when Paige was standing so close and looking so lovely. He'd told her sister the truth—Paige *was* always beautiful to him—but that didn't stop him from noting just how spectacularly stunning she looked tonight.

Still, he had a job to do, and he wasn't about to ruin the evening for everyone on Walker Island by blowing his lines.

"Ladies and gentlemen, I'm just a visitor to Walker Island, but already I've started to see how special things are here, and I'm amazed by the way this community has taken me into its arms." One beautiful member of that community in particular, he thought to himself. "But since I know you haven't come out here to listen to me talk, why don't we get started with the tree lighting? Can I get a countdown? Five, four, three, two, one!"

When they all got to *one*, he threw the big switch the island commission had provided, and lights went on around the harbor in a blaze of neon colors. Christian couldn't help looking back at Paige again, watching the way the different shades of light gleamed from her outfit and golden hair, making it seem like she was shining just like the lights.

He moved off to the side of the stage while the Walker sisters stepped forward. He found himself standing beside Michael, who had spent quite a lot of the day helping out with the rig for the lighting. Joel, Brian, and Nicholas were also nearby. Like Christian, they were dressed well for the occasion, but nothing like the incredible outfits the Walker sisters were wearing.

"They're beautiful, aren't they?" Michael said to him as, one by one, the five sisters used tapers to light the candles set around the tree. Christian could see the way Michael's eyes followed Emily as she did her part. Just the way Brian watched Morgan. And the way that Joel and Nicholas watched Hanna and Rachel, respectively. Christian was sure that each of the four men would have done *anything* for the woman he loved. They looked at the Walker sisters who had come into their lives with love that bordered on reverence.

Just the way he knew his own eyes followed Paige.

Would the people in the crowd be able to identify that look? Would they be able to tell what he felt for her as he stood there in front of them? Would they see just how amazing Paige was to him?

As Paige and her sisters finished lighting all the candles, Joel stepped up on stage first, moving over to Hanna and taking her hand so that they could walk down into the big Christmas Eve party together. Someone in the audience called out that it was the first time that a Walker and a Peterson had been to a Christmas Eve party together in fifty years, and the crowd cheered.

Nicholas went next, taking Rachel's hand. Brian followed to escort Morgan, and Michael moved to accompany Emily. She looked at him questioningly for a moment before putting her hand in his and joining the small procession with him.

Christian saw his moment and stepped up onto the stage, holding out his hand as though he was about to ask Paige to dance with him. She smiled briefly, then reached out to take it with the smooth grace that was such an integral part of her. The crowd cheered for the two of them the way they'd cheered all the others.

They probably thought that Christian was doing the same thing Michael had—filling in for one of the Walker sisters without a partner. He hoped Paige knew he didn't see it that way at all as he led her toward the rest of the party.

Ordinarily, he tried to avoid big parties like

this, both because people expected him to play the star and because of the threat of cameras recording his every move. Today was different, though.

He stopped under a small decorative arch that was surprisingly private in the midst of so many people so that he could speak to Paige alone for a moment. "Where there's music, there will be dancing."

She looked surprised, but not at all displeased by his statement. "You really want to dance here? In front of everyone?"

"There's no one I would rather dance with. And no place I'd rather be. Although there is one thing I want to do first."

"What's that?"

Christian smiled again and glanced up at the small archway where they'd stopped.

An archway that had a sprig of mistletoe pinned to it.

* * *

Before Paige could tell him—or even think of—all the reasons that they shouldn't do this again, Christian kissed her.

Their last kiss had been surprising, full of excitement and energy. This kiss was sweet and slow and absolutely perfect. She'd never been kissed with this kind of passion, or so much emotion.

When he gently stroked her cheek with his hand and drew back to look into her eyes, it was all Paige could do to keep from blurting out everything she felt for him and all the impossible things that she wished could come true for them.

Instead, she said, "We can't dance together tomorrow."

He looked at her in surprise. "Why not?"

Because she knew that if they danced together again, then there was no way she would be able to keep from declaring her love for him like a total idiot with stars in her eyes.

"What I mean is that you should take Christmas Day off. We both should. You've been working really hard."

"But there's still a lot to get through, isn't there?"

"We'll get to it," Paige assured him. Why did he have to be such a diligent student? Anyone else would have jumped at the opportunity to have a day away from working so hard.

"I knew what I was getting into when I came here," he insisted. "Besides, it's not exactly a chore dancing with you, Paige."

"But it will be Christmas Day," Paige countered with a smile. "You should go see your family and hug those nieces of yours, even if you're only there for a few hours. I don't want to be the ogre who's responsible for keeping their uncle away."

And it would also mean that she could have a whole day to recover from the feelings that kissing Christian had brought up. Both of them clearly needed to take a step back to try to think straight again.

"I do want to see them," Christian admitted, "but I want to be with you, too."

"Your family is more important than dance practice. It's more important than this movie, too."

"I agree, but it's not more important than y—"

Paige tried to cut him off before he said too much, but this time he wouldn't let her.

"You must already know how I feel about you. Me not saying it aloud won't change that." But instead of pushing her further, he said, "I'll go see my family tomorrow, since you're right, I really do want to see them on Christmas Day. But believe me, Paige, when I get back, the first thing I'll want to do is see you. Because there's no one else I'd rather be with. And I hope that between now and then you change your mind about letting me into your life."

CHAPTER FOURTEEN

Wrapping paper. Whoever invented it, Paige decided as she hurried to wrap presents for her family, had a sadistic streak.

Or maybe they'd designed it for people who weren't constantly thinking about Christian Greer.

Paige had set her alarm for five a.m. so she could get up ahead of everyone else to get her wrapping done. Why, oh, why did she do this to herself every darned year? It wasn't like putting things off—or shoving them into the back of her mind—ever made them any easier.

Just as she couldn't find a way to stop thinking about what Christian had said. Had he been serious about her being the person he most wanted to be with? And was he really waiting and hoping that she'd let him into her life, too?

Last night, she'd ended up feeling as if she'd lost her best friend. She'd walked home alone, knowing everyone else would be at the party for a long time to come. As soon as she'd gotten home, she'd slipped off the festive dress and carefully removed Morgan's makeup efforts, too, because as wonderful as they were, they couldn't last.

She had felt like Cinderella, home well before her coach turned into a pumpkin. And without her Prince Charming. All because she'd sent him away.

She'd tried to turn off the wildly careening thoughts in her brain by settling down in front of the TV, but when *Shall We Dance* started to play, she'd realized nothing was the same as it had been before Christian had burst into her life earlier that week. Before she'd met him, the movie had always brought memories of going through the steps with her mother. But now she'd spent too many hours rehearsing those same steps with Christian. Learning the way he felt when he was holding her in his arms and the wonderful way he moved. And experiencing an intimacy far greater than anything a movie, or fantasy, could ever provide.

Paige couldn't even see Fred and Ginger on the screen anymore. Instead, it was her and Christian on the screen dancing together...and then kissing passionately, utterly wrapped up in each other.

She knew then that it wasn't going to be easy to forget about Christian Greer. She could watch this film a dozen more times, a hundred more times, and it would still be his face that she saw in her head. And his kisses that she relived in her dreams.

Paige was so lost in her thoughts about him that when she looked down, she was momentarily surprised to see the pile of wrapped gifts in front of her. She hoped Emily would be happy with the large, glossy cookbooks she had chosen for her. For Rachel, she had purchased a couple's gift certificate to one of the island's spas. She'd chosen a beautiful coat for Morgan. And for Hanna, an attachment for one of her cameras that Paige knew she'd been drooling over online. Charlotte got a small climbing helmet, which had been the most awkward one to wrap. Then there were gifts for Grams, her father, Joel, Brian, Nicholas, and Michael.

Bending down to scoop up the gifts, she made her way downstairs. There wasn't a lot of room left under the tree, but she spread things out and then, exhausted, flopped down on the sofa to rest for a little while.

A couple of hours later she was wakened by Charlotte who, as always, was rummaging around under the tree trying to guess at the contents of the presents. Although, to be fair, Morgan was the real expert in that department.

The rest of the family arrived throughout the day, and they spent the next few hours sipping mimosas and hot chocolate. Everyone was excited and happy, and Paige felt so blessed to have not only such a wonderful family, but to know that so many of her sisters had found such great men with whom to start their own families. It was a perfect morning.

Well, *almost* perfect. Because Paige couldn't stop constantly wondering what Christian was doing. Had he managed to get a flight to the mainland last night? Was he having a good time with his family?

And did he miss her as much as she missed him?

"We need all hands on deck to get this place cleaned up and get the turkey in the oven," Emily called out after looking at her watch. With that, everyone pitched in, and pretty soon the family room was looking really good.

Paige took the chance to head upstairs and get showered and changed for their big family dinner this evening, which would be followed by opening gifts. When she had finished slipping into one of her prettiest dresses—a dark pink long-sleeved dress that nipped in at the waist then floated around her calves whenever she moved— she headed back down to set the table and peel vegetables.

As she walked down the stairs, she could hear the voices of her family from all corners of the house. Christmas carols were playing on the stereo, and everyone was clearly having a great time. With more than a tinge of regret, she wished that she hadn't shooed Christian off yesterday. He would have loved being here.

Morgan caught up with her just as she

stepped into the living room. "I thought you were never coming back down. Christian is in the kitchen helping Emily make cranberry sauce. He wanted to see you, but I told him you'd be down in a few minutes."

Christian was back already? Why hadn't he stayed with his own family? And could Emily really be letting someone else pitch in with the cranberry sauce?

Yet even as part of her was gripped by panic at seeing him again so soon, there was an even bigger part of her that was *incredibly* thankful to know that he was here.

The moment she walked through the kitchen door, he smiled at her and said, "Merry Christmas, Paige."

She could hardly find her voice, she was so happy to see him. "Merry Christmas, Christian." Feeling at a total loss—wanting to say a hundred different things at once to him, but too scared to actually say a single one—all that she ended up saying next was, "Cranberry sauce?"

"It's my specialty. It was the only thing my mother trusted me to make when I was a kid."

His sweet comment helped her get her brain in order, enough at least to say, "I'm amazed you got back to the island in time for dinner."

"I couldn't miss being with you," he said so softly that only she could hear him. "A quick flight last night, Christmas morning with my family, and then back here."

He made it sound so simple, but in reality it

was hours of exhausting traveling. All so he could see his family and then come back to spend Christmas night with her.

Just then, a tablet on the counter dinged. "Sorry," he said with an apologetic smile before he swiped a finger across the screen. "Okay, I think we're on. Can you hear me, Mom?"

"Of course I can hear you. I may be getting old, but I'm not losing my hearing quite yet," she joked. "Now, let me see where you are. Ah, the kitchen. Glad to see that they're making you earn your keep, at least."

Christian smiled down at the screen. "Yes, Mom. I'm making cranberry sauce."

"So the Walkers won't let you at the real food, either. Good for them. Did you tell them about the time you almost poisoned your sister trying to make cookies?"

Christian laughed. "I figured they wouldn't want to eat the cranberry sauce if I mentioned that. Besides, Janet's fine."

"She was so glad you were able to be with us for Christmas morning. I know it was just a short visit, but at least you were able to celebrate with everyone."

"You can thank Paige for that."

"I was hoping you would introduce me so that I can do just that."

Christian turned the tablet to face Paige so that she could see his mother peering into her webcam with a broad smile. "Mom, this is Paige. Paige, this is my mother, Angie."

"Finally, I'm meeting the woman my son couldn't stop talking about!"

More than a little stunned to hear his mother say that, Paige took a beat longer than it should have to say, "Hello, Angie. It's lovely to meet you."

"It's lovely to finally meet you, too, Paige. And I must say, you're every bit as lovely as he said you are. Now, don't you let my son shy away from his dancing. When he was young, if there was something he didn't want to do, he'd wander off into the garden and start acting all by himself instead."

"Mom!" Christian protested.

Angie laughed. "What are mothers for if not to embarrass their sons?"

Paige couldn't help laughing, too, despite the fact that she was still reeling from the fact that Christian had not only just introduced her to his mother, but had evidently been talking about her all day, too. At the same time, she couldn't help envying the relationship he had with his mother. If her own mom had been alive, would she be telling Christian all about what Paige was like when she was a kid? And would she be there to give Paige relationship advice?

"Paige used to go off to the dance studio and practice routines whenever there were chores," Emily supplied from behind them, obviously happy to fill in on behalf of their mother.

As Christian continued to work on his cranberry sauce, he was given some very vocal suggestions from his mother. "Raspberry vinegar? Are you sure you should add that, honey?"

Paige smiled at the thought that even big stars had mothers they had to please.

Soon his mother signed off to finish her own big holiday meal and the Walker table was loaded up with food, and every available space and chair were pressed into service. Tonight, even the large Walker dining room barely had enough room for everyone.

Paige sat next to Christian at dinner, and he was as charming and funny as he had been the first time he'd come to the house, but this time he seemed to fit in more naturally. It was as if he had been attending Walker family dinners for years. It felt so right to have him there with all of them.

"This is really nice," he said to Paige about halfway through the meal. "I'm so glad to be here."

Paige wanted to tell him how much she'd missed him even in the short time he'd been gone, but with her family all around them, she knew she'd have to wait. All she could say now was, "I'm glad you're here, too."

Dinner lasted a couple of hours, and everyone had double helpings of Emily's Christmas pudding. And then, finally, it was time to open the presents. Everyone gathered round the tree to start unwrapping their gifts, and it was only as Charlotte and Morgan tore into the first pieces of wrapping paper with equal enthusiasm that Paige realized one crucial thing.

"I'm sorry, Christian. I thought you'd be with your family all day. I didn't get you a gift."

"You've let me join your family for the day, you've given up most of the holidays to teach me to dance, and you've made me feel really welcome here on the island. Those are the best gifts I've ever had."

And then he was suddenly holding out a small package. She felt like a young girl again as she ripped open the packaging and saw that he'd bought her a DVD of the 1970 movie *Santa Claus Is Comin' to Town*.

"I figured that since there isn't any dancing, and Fred Astaire just does a voice-over, you might not have it."

Paige didn't, and it was incredibly sweet of him to think of it. She looked around to see that the rest of her family were just finishing unwrapping their presents. "Maybe we could watch it right now."

"I'd love that." Christian glanced around at her family. "But won't everyone else think it's a bit strange if we head off together?"

Paige smiled. "You've obviously never been to a Walker family Christmas before."

After the big family dinner and the communal unwrapping, everyone usually drifted off into their own corners of the house for a while to do their own thing. That had been true back when it had just been the sisters, their grandmother, and their father, but it was doubly so now. Hanna and Joel went off together first. Rachel, Nicholas, and

Charlotte all followed not long after. Brian and Morgan got deep into a conversation with Grams about their spring wedding. Their father started talking to Michael about some changes he was planning in his apartment. Emily soon joined in to brainstorm something similar she wanted done with the house, and of course, Michael looked more than happy to oblige.

Which left Paige and Christian free to head to the family room and turn on the movie. Their wonderful little ritual. But at the same time, now that they were finally alone, she wondered if he would want an answer now as to whether she was ready to have him in her life for more than just this one week.

"It's all right, Paige." When Christian reached out to stroke her hair, she knew he had read her mind. "I know I put too much pressure on you when I said I was going to come back looking for answers. I don't want to push you into more than you're ready for. I just can't deny what I feel and hope that you won't deny what you're feeling, either. But for tonight, let's just enjoy being together. No pressure. No big questions. No big answers. Just a perfect Christmas night in each other's arms. Although there is one thing I would like before we begin watching the movie."

He didn't have to say anything more, not when she wanted the very same thing. And as she pressed her lips to his in a kiss that danced from gentle to passionate in the span of a heartbeat, she knew she'd never had a more perfect

Christmas in her life.

A short while later, they were curled up together on the couch under a blanket, watching the movie. The animated film was a lot of fun, but all of the ups and downs of the last couple of days had worn her out, and with Christian's arms so warm and strong around her, Paige shut her eyes. Just for a moment or two...

* * *

Her eyes flickered open what felt like a moment later. Christian was as asleep as she had been, his arms wrapped around her as though to try to keep out the rest of the world.

It was a beautiful feeling, being held by him. So beautiful that, as his eyes opened, too, Paige remained perfectly still, wanting the moment to last. It felt so safe, but so fragile, too, as though they both knew that they would soon have to move, and then the moment would fade.

Early morning light filtered through the windows onto the pair of them, and she finally realized that though she'd meant to shut her eyes only for a moment, she'd spent all night in Christian's arms.

That thought was enough to make Paige move like greased lightning. "We've got to get down to the studio." She was on her feet in a flash. "This is our last full day of practice. After this, we may only be able to steal a few hours in the studio here and there."

He got to his feet, too, but before he did

anything else, he put his hands on either side of her face and kissed her. "Now, that," he said in a loving tone that warmed her inside and out, "is a proper good morning."

And as she let herself forget about dancing for another few moments as she kissed him, Paige knew that it was better than any other morning she'd ever had before.

CHAPTER FIFTEEN

Knowing today was their last full day of practice where they could work together uninterrupted for hours on end brought with it a whole host of thoughts and feelings, from the question of whether they'd managed to get in enough dance instruction so far, to a vague sense of relief that the frantic pace would relax a little after today, to the tight knot in Paige's stomach at knowing Christian would soon be leaving.

On top of it all, he'd just reminded her that the entertainment news crew would be arriving at the studio this morning to get some publicity footage.

"Do you think I'm ready to show off my dancing skills?" he said as they headed to the studio.

"Without a doubt," she told him, giving him a big smile so that he hopefully wouldn't see just how nervous *she* was about having so many people around with cameras, watching them practice, and asking questions. But today wasn't about her. It was about making sure Christian shone in front of the cameras, and she would do absolutely everything in her power to make sure that happened.

As she pulled into a parking spot in front of the dance studio and grabbed her bag, she tried to sound casual as she said, "So *who* exactly is coming today?"

"I doubt the entertainment shows will send any big reporters, given that most of them are likely taking some time off with their families over the holidays, but there will probably be at least a couple of people looking for live interviews and at least one photographer taking still shots. Oh, and I've just heard this morning that our choreographer, Lynn, will be there, as well."

Oh God, today had too quickly turned from a practice session into a performance, and Paige didn't perform. *Ever.* But she made herself force another smile anyway. One that Christian clearly wasn't buying, unfortunately.

He took her hands in his and drew her closer. "Don't worry, Paige. It's just normal movie publicity. They won't get in the way. It will just be you and me dancing like normal." She could tell from his soothing tone that he knew how nervous she was, even if he hadn't guessed all the reasons.

As they walked toward the studio, Paige was surprised to see Morgan standing at the door, looking immaculate and glossy, the way she would have for a meeting with one of the TV executives.

"I'm here to help out," her sister said before she could even say good morning or ask why she was there. "I had a message from the studio late last night asking if I could do makeup for the shoot. So here I am! How about if we go to the locker rooms so I can do your makeup for you while you get changed? I was thinking of doing something similar to the way you looked the other night at the tree ceremony. You looked amazing, and it would look perfect on-screen."

"Paige always looks amazing," Christian said with a smile. "Just the way she does right now."

"Thank you for saying that," she said to him, before turning to her sister. "Thank you for offering to do my makeup, but I'd rather practice today with everything the same as it's been."

As she went to get changed, Morgan followed her. "Are you sure?"

"Completely sure. But it really was nice of you to come."

"Well, even if you don't need me to make you up, I'm happy to help out with answering any questions the crew might have while you're practicing and directing them to the nearest coffee shop. Besides, my day is already made just from seeing you and Christian together again. Did you and he...?"

"No!"

"I'm not blind, you know."

Paige started to pull on her dance clothes. "I know, but it's just... it's complicated."

"Things are always complicated," Morgan pointed out. "But lots of times they work out, too. Just look at me and Brian."

Paige wished it were that simple. After all, her sister had been in love with Brian since they'd been kids. Of course they could overcome anything that came their way. "I just can't think about anything but dancing today. I've got to make sure Christian looks good dancing on camera so that everyone will see how well he's going to do in the movie."

"Just promise me you won't get so involved in the dancing that you forget about everything else."

Knowing her sister wouldn't leave it alone until she agreed, Paige said, "I promise."

"Good," Morgan said with a wide smile. "Now, I'll go and say hello to the film crew since they pulled up just behind you and Christian. I'm sure they'll probably want to interview both of you, so I'll help them find a good place to set up their equipment that won't be in your way while you're dancing."

By the time Paige finished getting changed and headed into the studio, sure enough, the practice space was packed with equipment from both the film crews and the photographers. Christian was speaking with a woman in her fifties who Paige immediately guessed was the choreographer from nothing more than the smooth, delicate grace of her gestures. Plus, she'd tied back her gray-streaked auburn hair in the same style Paige always did. Although, today, Paige had left her hair loose.

"Paige, come meet our choreographer, Lynn."

She shook the other woman's hand, and as she did so, she could see some of the same spark in the woman's eyes that Grams had.

"It's lovely to meet you. I was so glad when I heard that Christian was taking lessons before we start official rehearsals. It will be great to see how far you've been able to get this week."

Paige could hear the excuse the choreographer was offering her: that a week was obviously too short a time to be able to do much in terms of training. It was kind, but she knew Christian didn't need excuses...and she had also decided that there was no way she was going to let her own fears of dancing in front of the cameras and choreographer get in the way of the job Christian had put his faith in her to do.

"Lynn, it is really a pleasure to meet you. I've heard so many great things about you over the years that it's great to put a face to a name." With a smile for Christian, she said, "Are you ready to get warmed up?"

A short while later, when they were both feeling loose and ready to dance, Paige cued up the music. Christian moved smoothly out into the middle of the floor, offering her his hand. Paige smiled at him, took his hand, and they began to go through the steps they'd been working on. If the camera crews thought they would just go through a couple of pieces for their benefit, they were wrong. Paige wasn't about to cheat Christian's practice time, no matter who was here. Fortunately, she already knew how good his dancing was going to look through the camera lens. Because it had turned out that Christian Greer was a natural.

As he danced close to her, she was pleased by the way he brilliantly used his acting ability and charisma to make up for any technique that was still a little rough. But more than that, she was glad to feel how strong the connection between them was as they danced. Two days ago, when Grams had walked in during their practice session, that connection had seemed so broken and stilted. But today, they were moving in perfect sync as Christian led her around the floor.

"That was great," Paige said as they finished. "Let's try the second half again."

"My shoulders?" Christian guessed.

"Your posture's good," Paige assured him. "I just want to get those last couple of turns a little crisper."

So they kept dancing, and as they did, it was surprisingly easy to forget the whirring cameras, bright lights, and assistants taking notes and sending text messages. Instead, it felt like it was just the two of them...and that dancing with Christian was the only thing that mattered.

Finally, they broke apart for a rest, and the others in the room took that as a cue to move in, with Morgan leading the way.

"That was amazing, Paige." Morgan gave her a quick hug, before adding, "The crew would like to get a couple of interviews during the break. Will that work for you?"

"Sure. It would be good for Christian to get off his feet for a bit since he's been working so hard this morning. I'll just make myself scarce in the office."

Morgan smiled at her. "They'd like to interview you, too, actually." And that was how Paige suddenly found herself in front of a camera being asked what it was like to work with such a famous, gorgeous actor.

"It's kind of hard to remember sometimes that he's a star when he's a few inches away, dancing with me," she explained. "Honestly, we're just trying to get the job done, and he's been working very, very hard."

After a few easy dance questions, the interviewer asked, "What would you say to all the women who think that you've got a dream job, getting to dance with Christian Greer?"

Oh God, she thought. What if her answer accidentally gave away her feelings for him to the entire world?

Fortunately, right then, Christian interrupted them. "Paige, one of the crews has asked if we can do an interview with you dancing in the background."

She tried to swallow down her panic at dancing in front of the cameras without him. "Are you sure that wouldn't look a bit odd?"

"Are you kidding?" He looked truly surprised by her question. "It would be amazing. Will you do it? Please?"

How could Paige deny him anything when he asked her so sweetly?

After she nodded, he said, "Great, thank you. I'll get the music started." A few moments later, the music from *They All Laughed* began. "Just dance it the way you did the other night."

With the cameras already rolling, there was no time to protest, so she simply danced the version with her choreography, moving seamlessly from the traditional steps to modern jazz. Feeling Christian's eyes on her the whole time, even as he was being interviewed, she was shocked by how easy it was to focus only on him and not worry about anyone else. And then, suddenly, he moved away from the cameras. Paige had been dancing Astaire's part for the first section, but he moved smoothly in to take the lead.

Oh my. It was *so* wonderful to dance with him, like all of her fantasies and dreams were finally coming true, every time he held her in his arms.

Finally, he expertly spun her to a stop. Paige stood, breathing hard and looking into his eyes as he stared into hers. For a moment, she thought he might kiss her, but he seemed to remember the film crews just in time.

"So," Christian said as he turned to the crowd filming them, "did you get everything you need?"

Just looking at the faces of the crew, Paige knew that they had. Even so, there were still more interview questions for Christian to answer. Clearly, this wasn't going to be a normal day of practice, after all.

Paige moved to the wall to wait for them to finish, grabbing her bottle of water and throwing a towel around her shoulders. Lynn, the choreographer, joined her.

"You've made my job a whole lot easier," Lynn said. "Thank you."

"It's been my pleasure. But you should know that Christian has worked very hard."

"I'm sure he has, but you still got more out of him in a week than most people would have in a month. And then there's that incredible version of *They All Laughed*. Is that your choreography?"

"It's just something I was playing around with."

"It's good. Really good. In fact, we've been talking about updating the dance styles for the movie. We could use some of that choreography."

"I'm sure you must have plenty of ideas," Paige said politely, but inside the thought that Lynn might actually want to use her work was very flattering.

"Trust me, Paige, I'm one of the toughest critics around. So when I see something that blows me away, I'm not about to let it go. Plus, you clearly have a great connection with Christian. It would be great to have you around for the shoot. You don't have to give me an answer now. I'll just have my agent talk to your agent."

It was the most amazing opportunity of her life, but somehow all Paige could manage was, "I don't have an agent."

"How about your sister's agent then? I'm sure he'd take you on. And since you *do* have such a good connection with Christian," the choreographer continued, "perhaps you could do me a huge favor? There's a charity dance that he's booked to take part in on New Year's Eve. In the absence of his co-star, I was going to fill in, but the two of you are magic together." Lynn looked her straight in the eye as she added, "As close to the magic of Fred and Ginger that I've seen."

CHAPTER SIXTEEN

As soon as Christian finished his final interview, he pulled Paige back onto the dance floor. "I'm so glad I almost have you to myself again," he whispered in her ear, sending thrill bumps all across her body. After he whirled and spun her until her heart was fluttering like crazy, he drew her close again and said, "You were amazing today in front of the cameras. Were you okay with it?"

"Actually," she admitted, "I forgot about the cameras pretty fast."

He studied her face for a moment. "But that's not why you look so happy is it?"

All but bursting to tell him the news, she said, "Lynn wants to use some of my choreography in the film!"

Christian looked down at her with an intensity that made Paige's heart thrum in her chest. Pressed so tightly to him, she was sure that he must be able to feel it.

"Did you say yes?" When she nodded, he said, "That's incredible, Paige. I'm so happy for you. And not at all surprised."

"I am," she said honestly, "but not just because of that. Lynn also asked if I would dance at a charity dinner at New Year's with you, too."

His face lit up even more upon hearing that. "There's no one I'd rather dance with. I know you've always preferred being backstage and helping others shine, but you're the most beautiful dancer I've ever seen. And you just said it yourself, how quickly you forgot about the cameras today. I'll bet you'll forget about the audience at the charity gala even faster."

Her nerves were still there, but his very sweet and comforting words helped push them down...for the time being, anyway. Enough that she was able to tease, "Just wait until you meet your co-star. One dance with her, and you'll forget all about your lessons with me."

"I don't care if she wins the championship a dozen times. It's not just about the dancing, Paige. You *know* it's not. And I would *never* forget about you."

The next thing she knew, Christian had put his hands on either side of her face, and he was kissing her.

In front of a room full of people!

She knew they had already turned the cameras off and were just finishing packing up their equipment into the vans, but even so, for him to kiss her in public... Paige should have been as terrified by that thought as she was by the idea of dancing with him in public on New Year's!

Amazingly, though, she could feel herself getting swept up in the passion of the kiss instead.

Her life felt as perfect as it had ever been. Christian had progressed perfectly with the dancing that he had come to Walker Island to learn. She'd just been offered an amazing opportunity as a choreographer, *and* Christian was kissing her.

Feeling as if she was living in a dream—and not wanting to ever wake up from it—she resolutely refused to dwell on the public performance coming up in a few days. Or the fact that Christian practically lived twenty-four/seven in the spotlight when he wasn't hiding out for a week on a small island in the Pacific Northwest learning to dance.

After saying good-bye to the interviewers, film crews, and photographers, they laughed and danced, taking the steps that they'd worked on and turning them into something lighter as they moved together. She wanted to savor every moment of being with Christian like this, but she knew she ought to call a halt to practice.

"What should we do for dinner?" she asked. "Grab Chinese again?"

Christian continued to hold her close. "I was thinking of something a little fancier tonight. How would you like to join me at one of the restaurants down on the waterfront?"

"I'd love to, but I'm sure they'll all be booked solid by now."

"Trust me," he said with a smile. "I'll find a spot for us."

"If we're going somewhere like that, then I should go home to change." The last thing she wanted was to embarrass him by looking like something the cat dragged in.

He kissed her again before saying, "It doesn't matter what you're wearing. You're always the most beautiful woman in the room."

Even so, Paige headed to the studio's locker rooms to shower and put on her street clothes. She'd just finished dressing when Morgan burst in and threw her arms around her.

"I was just about to leave when I saw the two of you kissing! You and Christian are *perfect* together! I'm so happy for you. Now, hold still while I do your makeup. And, no arguing. You already ducked out of this once today. And you know it's my dream come true to get to make you up more than once a year."

This time, Paige let her sister work her magic. And when Morgan was done, Paige took a look at herself and couldn't stop a small gasp of pleasure. She was wearing much less makeup than she had on Christmas Eve, but she still could hardly believe how deftly her sister had transformed her with only a little blush, mascara, and lipstick.

"Have fun," Morgan said, pushing her out in the direction of the studio.

Christian was waiting for her already, looking as gorgeous as ever in his street clothes. "Like I said, you're the most beautiful woman in the world."

Flushed with pleasure, she loved the way he took her hand as they headed out into the crisp evening air. Later, the stars would be out, shining brightly. For now, it was enough to feel as if *she* was shining beside Christian.

They walked down to the harbor, and he led them through the doors of a small Asian fusion restaurant with an upper balcony that had a clear view out over the water. No one seemed to care that the two of them were dressed casually. In fact, their waiter even commented on how beautiful Paige looked that evening.

Paige smiled at that, knowing it was because she was all but glowing with happiness. "I love the restaurant you chose for us. I can't believe you found us a table. It's packed tonight!"

"They were more than happy to help out a couple of starved dancers."

"That's very kind of them, although I suspect they also wanted to be able to tell their friends that Christian Greer ate in their restaurant."

He looked at her seriously. "Do you mind?"

She was surprised to find that she didn't. Not then. Not when it meant they could spend time alone together having a romantic dinner after a day that had already been perfect in almost every conceivable way.

"No, I don't mind at all."

"I'm glad because, believe me, none of that matters right now."

"What does matter to you, Christian?" she asked in a voice that was just a little huskier than normal.

"You do, Paige." He reached for her hand and stroked his thumb across her palm, sending more thrill bumps across her skin. "Just you."

And though the restaurant had a spectacular view, Christian kept his eyes on her the whole time they were eating dinner. His hand also reached out to brush hers more than once as they ate, and she found that she could barely remember what she'd ordered or eaten. But just as he'd said, right then none of that mattered.

Only him.

When they stepped outside after dinner, the stars were just starting to come out, clear pinpoints of light against the blackness. Paige walked beside Christian, snuggling close to him against the cool of the night air. They walked past bars and restaurants and houses where parties were still going, music spilling out into the night.

Christian held his hand out to her. "Dance with me."

Unable to resist, she took his hand, and he pulled her smoothly into a waltz as naturally as if they'd been dancing together beneath the starlight their entire lives. When she realized he was leading them back toward her house, she shook her head.

"Let's go to your hotel tonight."

He paused then, holding her tightly in his arms. "Are you sure?"

"Yes." She'd never been more sure about anything in her life.

They were all propriety and decorum as they walked past the man at the front desk, but the elevator was another matter. Christian kissed her passionately as they traveled upward, breaking off just in time when an older woman got in. She looked at them suspiciously until they reached Christian's floor. Paige managed to keep a straight face until the elevator doors closed behind them, but then had to bury her face against Christian's chest to keep from laughing too loud.

"Are you absolutely sure about this, Paige?" he asked again a few moments later. "I know how easy it is to get caught up in the moment, but I want our first time together to be more than that. So much more."

Of course she was caught up in the moment. How could she not be after a day like this? Yet Paige knew that it was more than that. She wanted—*needed*—to be with him. Even closer than they'd already been on the dance floor.

So much closer.

"Does this answer your question?" she said as she closed the door to his suite and began to rain kisses all along his jaw.

He stroked her hair, brushing it away from her face as he traced a soft line of kisses along her cheekbones. And then he was lifting her with the same ease he'd used all week during practice and carrying her to the bedroom to lay her down in the center of the bed.

"You're so beautiful, Paige. So lovely you take my breath away."

"You're sweet, but you don't have to keep saying that."

"Why don't you believe me when I tell you how beautiful you are?"

"Because I've always been the forgettable one in my family."

He touched her cheek, bringing her eyes up to meet his. "Trust me, there is no way that anyone could ever forget you."

And when he kissed her again with such sweet passion—and emotion that felt wonderfully deep and true—she finally let herself believe that he meant every word he said.

CHAPTER SEVENTEEN

Paige blinked her way back to wakefulness slowly and dreamily, smiling as memories of last night came flooding back. She was in Christian's hotel suite after a night that had been...

Her smile broadened as she thought of the perfect word: *magical.* Their night together had been simply *magical.*

She could hear him on the phone in the other room and decided to leave the bed to join him. When he saw her walk in, wrapped only in a sheet, Paige wasn't sure which she loved more—his gorgeous and welcoming smile or the way his eyes moved heatedly over her.

"Good morning," she whispered.

He told his caller to hold on for a moment and then kissed her. A "proper good morning" as he liked to call it...and she had to agree that it was the perfect way to start the day. Their kiss was sweet and lingering, the way so much of their lovemaking had been, but eventually Christian had to break it off to go back to his phone call.

"It's my agent," he explained in an apologetic voice, but Paige could understand that he wasn't truly on vacation while on the island, even if a part of her wanted to toss his phone aside and pull him back in the direction of the bedroom.

She sat beside him instead. His gaze never left her as he spoke to his agent, and he couldn't seem to stop running his hand over her hair and across her bare shoulder, either. She quite liked the idea of being able to distract the likes of Christian Greer, she thought with a grin she didn't bother to hold back.

And then, suddenly, something his agent said clearly surprised him. "That's what they really said? That the part's mine if I want it?" He kissed Paige again, a quick, and very happy, kiss. "It's a lead role in a big fantasy movie," he explained in a whisper with his hand over the receiver.

"Congratulations," she whispered back as she squeezed his hand tight. "I'm so happy for you."

He made a sign to her with his fingers that he was planning to wrap up his call immediately so that they could celebrate. "It all sounds great," he told his agent. "I've got to get going now, so why don't you get the contracts in place and make sure they send me an early copy of the script? Although since I've never used a sword before, we're going to have to find a sword-fighting instructor." Christian listened for a moment and then smiled at Paige again. "They think that because I did such a quick job of learning to dance, I'll learn to sword fight in no time? That's great." He mouthed a quick *thank you* to Paige before going back to finishing his phone call.

"Why don't you get in touch with that woman who worked on that HBO series playing a wandering swordswoman? Zana Lizski, I think. I'm pretty sure she choreographed a lot of the sword work." He paused as he listened to his agent on the other end. "I've really enjoyed being Paige's student. Hopefully, I can have just as pleasurable an experience with Zana."

Paige managed to keep smiling. Barely. In that moment, though, it was all she could do not to run to the bathroom to be sick. She'd known all along, of course, that when the remake of *Shall We Dance* was finished filming, Christian would go off to make another movie, giving it every ounce of his focus, the way he should. But hearing that he was going to get a sword-fighting instructor for his new movie?

Well, it was all she needed to hear to know that he was soon going to forget all about her...no matter what he'd said to the contrary.

As she got up on rubbery legs and headed back into the bedroom, she thought about the previous night when she'd been so sure that she was special to him. All week he'd made her feel special, but when they'd finally made love, it had been as if she was the only woman in the world who mattered to him. Yet he was already making arrangements to have exactly the same kind of one-on-one tutoring for his next movie.

Rationally, she knew that just because his possible sword-fighting instructor was a beautiful woman who had starred in a TV show didn't mean she would end up in his bed after a week of teaching him swordplay. The odds were that it wouldn't happen like that, when all was said and done.

Probably.

Most likely.

And yet...

That wasn't even really the point, was it? It didn't matter if Christian ended up getting romantic with his next instructor for his next film. What mattered was that there would *be* a next instructor. And that to him, even after last night, Paige would never ultimately be anything more than just the latest in a long line of teachers for the skills he needed to learn as an actor. He might have been temporarily infatuated with her, but he would soon be moving on. Gone, never to come back to Walker Island...or the girl who had so foolishly lost her heart to him in only one short week of dancing together.

The worst part of all was that she'd known it all along, but had been so swept up in the fantasy of being with him that she'd forced herself to push away reality.

Well, it looked like reality had just come storming back, whether she wanted it to or not.

Paige choked back the beginnings of tears, but they spilled down her cheeks anyway. She'd tried to remind herself throughout the week that Christian was too big a star and that letting him into her heart would be a mistake. Of course he was going to move on. His career as an actor was always going to demand that he should, and she would never ask him to give up his life for her.

She loved him too much to even dream of doing that.

When Patrice had left her all those years ago, she'd had nothing. Not him, not her dreams, not even her dignity. It had felt like tumbling into a black pit from which there was no way out. But she wouldn't fall apart like that again. After all, she was the one who had chosen to be with Christian last night—a night that she would never, ever regret—so she needed to be the one to suck it up and be a big girl about accepting that it would be their one and only time together.

Quickly wiping away her tears, she put on the clothes she'd worn last night and even took the time to tie her hair back neatly before stepping back into the other room, where Christian was just hanging up the phone.

He turned around, smiling at her. "I thought I was going to be coming in there after you, yet here you are dressed. What's wrong, sweetheart? Did you change your mind about lingering in bed a bit longer this morning?"

Paige simply nodded because she didn't trust herself to say anything.

"I know, you're right. If we went back to bed now, who knows when we might get back to the studio to squeeze in a little more practice? Of course, I'll be looking forward to tonight every single second we're dancing together today."

She tried to keep her voice steady. "We don't need to go back to the studio today."

"We don't?"

"No." Despite how hard she was trying to keep it together, her voice almost broke on the two-letter word, and she had to take a deep breath to continue. "Your lessons are complete."

"Paige." He moved closer, but she took a step back, knowing that if he touched her, she'd shatter into a million little pieces. "What's wrong?"

"I...I need to go now."

"Maybe you're right," he said slowly, and it felt as if her heart actually fell out of her chest to thud on the floor. "We should pack up and head out to LA today so that you can meet the rest of Lynn's choreography team before our dance at the charity gala. And my family, too. I'd love for you to meet them—and I know they'd love to meet you, too."

Oh God, she'd forgotten about the charity gala. And he was talking about her meeting his family? How could he not realize what a mistake that would be?

Paige felt dizzy with emotion as she said, "I'm not going to be able to dance with you in Los Angeles."

"Yesterday you said you'd love to do it." Christian's brow furrowed. "Why have you changed your mind?" He sounded not just confused, but hurt, too.

"I just can't do it."

"There *has* to be a reason." He reached for her again, and she wasn't quick enough to move away this time. She could feel his heart thudding fast and hard against hers as he said, "Tell me what's wrong. Five minutes ago you were glowing with happiness...and now you're as pale as a ghost. Did I do something to hurt you?"

No, he hadn't. Not yet. But he would when he left. So she needed to rip off the Band-Aid now instead of getting even deeper into his life by staying involved with his dancing and his movie.

"You can find another partner. Your choreographer, Lynn, could do it. Or your co-star, Liana, could take one day out of her world championship preparations. I'm sure she'd do a much better job at the charity dance than I could anyway."

"No one could do a better job than you, Paige."

She forced herself to step out of his arms. "Can't you see? That's just the problem. This is a *job*, Christian. Maybe we both forgot that for a night, but it doesn't change anything."

"You think last night didn't change things between us?"

"I *know* it didn't. You're still a big star, and I'm still just me."

"I know you have your reservations about the spotlight, but I would never let anyone hurt you,

Paige. *Never.* Please, at least give us some time to find a way to make things work. We don't have to go to LA today. We could just go to your studio to dance together, or watch another Fred Astaire movie, or—"

"I can't! Not when it feels like every time I do something with you, I get swept up. Swept completely away from reality! I dance with you, and it feels like there's nothing else in the world that matters. I go roller-skating with you, and I can't help but kiss you. I even danced on camera for your interviews, which is something I would never do for anyone else. When I'm with you, it's so easy just to go along with it all. But it isn't real, Christian. It's like we're in a movie, one where it feels like real life until the movie ends, and then you wake up to find that you're just sitting in a theater and nothing has changed. I..." Her throat hurt from trying so hard to hold back her tears in front of him. "I can't be there for the moment when you finally wake up and realize that someone else should be your leading lady. We had one amazing week together on this island, but we both know that's all it will ever be."

She made herself walk to the door, but couldn't leave without adding in a broken voice thick with unshed tears, "Good luck with the movie. I'll be rooting for you, every step of the way." Her tears began to fall again as she forced herself to say, "Good-bye, Christian," without running back into his arms.

CHAPTER EIGHTEEN

Ice cream.

Paige hoped ice cream would make everything better as she sat down on the couch in the living room with a bucketful. Something had to, and she'd gone to the store to get the biggest container it had, because some things needed more ice cream than others. Maybe there wasn't enough ice cream in the world to help her get over Christian, but she had to at least give it a try. Anything that might numb the pain she was feeling inside.

All morning long, she'd been telling herself that she'd done the right thing. That it was the only thing she could have done. Because sooner or later—emphasis on *sooner*—he would have found a woman far more suited to a star like him. And just because Paige had felt like the world was a better place every time they were close, just because she'd gotten so utterly swept up in everything they did together, didn't mean that Christian wouldn't wake up one day soon and wonder what spell he'd been under to fall for some nobody dance teacher from Walker Island.

"Focus on the ice cream," she reminded herself, even though it was almost noon and she had yet to have a proper breakfast.

Plenty of ice cream had always worked to make her and her sisters feel better when they were kids, although it had never really been Paige's preferred approach. The trouble was that neither of the options she usually went for when she was upset were available. Grams and Emily were out with Rachel, Charlotte, and Nicholas, enjoying more of the island's holiday festivities. So talking things through with them was out. And as for just heading down to the dance studio and dancing until she either felt better or collapsed...well, for today anyway, Paige had a pretty good idea which of those was likely to happen first. More to the point, she didn't feel like dancing, and that was a very strange new feeling in and of itself.

She *always* felt like dancing. Maybe not in front of anyone else, but she'd always craved the sensation of movement and the music running through her, making her a part of something that was bigger than any pain she might be feeling.

When her mother had died, she'd danced until she'd twisted an ankle and her father had had to carry her home to Grams' place. After Patrice had dumped her, she'd danced in Grams' studio until Emily had been ready to organize an intervention for her.

Today, though, she didn't want to dance. Not when she knew that there was no way she would be able to without thinking about Christian. Without imagining him there with her.

Which left her sitting on the couch with the creamy dessert she was quickly realizing after only one spoonful that she had absolutely no appetite for. Plus, she couldn't even watch one of her favorite dance movies, because just a glimpse would remind her that she'd spent so much of the last week foolishly falling head over heels for Christian.

So if not ice cream and a movie, what then? Before she could come up with another plan, Paige heard the sound of the front door opening.

"Is anyone home?"

She'd never been quite so happy to hear her father's voice. She dropped the ice cream container onto the table, then ran up and hugged him.

"What a wonderful hug." But when they drew back, and he finally saw her face, he said, "Oh, sweetheart, what's wrong?"

"Can't I just be happy to see you?"

It was obvious that her father could see right through her. As easily as he'd seen through her attempts to get out of her homework when she was a kid so she could get more time at the dance studio.

But knowing her better than almost anyone,

all he gently said for the time being was, "Of course you can. Are you home alone?"

"Everyone else is out," Paige explained. "I didn't know you were coming over, Dad."

"I thought I'd surprise you all."

But she could see through him, too. "And to see what kind of leftovers we have from the Christmas meal, maybe?" Her father coming over to grab leftovers was another of those family Christmas traditions. So when he laughed and nodded, she put her arm through his and said, "I'm sure there will be something in the refrigerator. Why don't we go and look?"

"That sounds good. And then you can tell me what has you so upset."

If she talked about it, she would only end up crying, and she didn't want to cry, not again. The whole point of walking away from Christian had been so that she wouldn't end up as some kind of tearful mess. And so that she wouldn't let another relationship reduce her to...well, this.

"I can't," she said softly.

"Well, then why don't we just watch some TV together for now?" her father suggested. "And then if you're in more of a talking mood later, we can chat."

Her father hadn't always been around when she and her sisters were kids—first, he'd been so busy working and then he'd been caught up with grief over the death of the girls' mother. But she knew he'd always done his best for them. Grams and Emily might have done a lot to bring them up, but as an adult, her father had always been there for her when it had really counted.

"TV sounds good."

"Do you want me to make you something for lunch?" he asked.

"I've got ice cream."

"That bad, huh?"

Paige shook her head again. "I'm fine."

Or, at least, she would be fine. Eventually. Even if it killed her.

They went and sat on the couch, turning on the TV. A Christmas show was on, but they switched to a wildlife documentary, and by that point quite a lot of the ice cream and leftovers seemed to have disappeared.

Paige would say this for her father: He knew precisely when to say nothing. And it really was enough for her that he was there, sitting beside her, eating what was left of the big family meal while watching a bunch of wildebeest tromp across the screen. It wasn't the same as having Christian there beside her, yet it was still far, far better than being alone.

The midday news came on next, and most of it was actually pretty upbeat, so neither of them changed the channel. Which turned out to be a *huge* mistake when the news anchor said, "In entertainment news, we recently caught up with Christian Greer, lead actor in the remake of the Astaire and Rogers classic *Shall We Dance.* Greer has been working hard in preparation for this role at a dance studio on an island outside Seattle.

He was kind enough to arrange for my colleagues to get some footage of his training."

When they cut to images of Christian dancing with her in the studio, Paige realized this was the first time she'd seen herself dancing with him. The first time in a very long time that she'd seen herself dancing at all, actually.

"Dad, can we change—"

"Shh, I want to watch you. It isn't every day that I get to see my beautiful daughter dancing on national television and know that everyone else is getting to see how talented you are, too."

"I don't think anyone but you is looking at me, Dad."

He raised an eyebrow. "Christian certainly wasn't looking anywhere else. And you weren't looking anywhere but at him, you know."

Paige started to deny that, but when she looked back at the TV, she was shocked to realize that her father was right. Not only was she looking at Christian as if he was the only man in the world, but, amazingly, he was looking at her in exactly the same way: with pure, sweet love.

She knew that, as an actor, he might be able to fake falling in love in a movie or TV show, but Paige had never been able to act like that. The love in her own eyes was utterly honest.

And, despite his acting skill, so was the love in his. Far more honest than she'd been with either of them when she'd run out of his hotel room, frightened beyond belief of how big her love for him was. Frightened of ever giving herself to anyone again. Foolishly thinking that she could somehow keep herself safe from ever being hurt again.

The news anchor went on. "Despite the incredible connection you've just witnessed between Christian and his dance partner, sources have been unable to confirm rumors of a romantic link. So don't worry, ladies, there's hope for you yet!"

"You know, Paige," her father said as he finally turned off the TV, "I've always loved seeing you dance. Watching you and Christian together reminds me of dancing with your mother when we were younger. Did I ever tell you about how I met her?" He didn't wait for a reply. "I was just starting out as a student teacher. I was kind of a nerd, and your mom was so far out of my league, I didn't ever really think she meant it when she said how much she liked spending time with me. But you know what your grandmother can be like when it comes to wanting to see two people with a spark be happy together. Your grandmother told me that men should learn to appreciate dance, and when I saw your mom dance for the first time, I knew that I was in love. She was such a beautiful, perfect, almost otherworldly creature. So graceful, and already the best dancer in school by a long shot."

Paige could easily imagine that. It was how she always remembered her mother, after all.

Her father went on. "So you can imagine how nervous I was. Ellen was so perfect and I...well, I was the guy any girl like that should have ignored. I wasn't handsome or special. I certainly didn't think that I could ever deserve someone like her."

"But you and Mom were perfect for one another! Of course you deserved her."

"That's what I had to learn, Paige. It's not about *deserving* someone. If it were, I'm sure your mother would probably have ended up with someone else. It wasn't about deserving her, it was about *loving* her. And finally getting up the nerve to actually ask her out. It took me most of a week to pluck up the courage to finally do it, and she told me afterwards that she'd been worried I wasn't going to ask when all along she'd been pining away for me the same way I had been for her." He peered at Paige through his glasses. "Do you understand what I'm trying to say, sweetheart?"

Paige understood perfectly. She'd spent so long wondering if she could ever be worthy of loving someone like Christian that she'd ignored the simple fact that she did love him. She'd pushed him away because she'd thought there was no chance they could ever make things work as a couple.

But that wasn't fair to either one of them, was it?

"What do I do, Dad?"

"What do you want to do?"

"I want to go to Christian and tell him that I made a big mistake. I want to tell him that I love him and that I was scared. I want to tell him I was wrong to push him away the way I did. But I'm sure he isn't even on the island anymore. There's this big charity dance in Los Angeles that I had said I was going to do with him tonight, but then I pulled out."

"If we head out immediately, I'm sure it wouldn't be that difficult to get to Los Angeles by this evening, would it?"

No, it wouldn't. Although Paige would have gone even if it had been a thousand times harder.

"I need to run upstairs to pack."

"Before you do..." Her father put his arms around her again and kissed the top of her head. "I know I don't always say it enough, but I'm proud of you, Paige, and I love you very, very much." He beamed down at her as he added, "And I'm so glad you've found a man who clearly loves and appreciates you as much as all of us do."

CHAPTER NINETEEN

Since arriving in Los Angeles, Christian had been home to see his family, he'd spoken to his agent about the new movie opportunity, he'd met his new co-star for *Shall We Dance*, and he'd been practicing with the movie's choreographer, Lynn, in a large downtown rehearsal space.

But none of it had helped to take his mind off Paige.

When he'd first been invited to be a part of the charity gala, Christian had been pleased to be able to help out the local community. He'd been doubly pleased to have Paige as his partner for the gala, because it would be the perfect way to show the whole world how much she meant to him.

But now, without her here, all he could feel was an aching loss. Especially when, with every step he took with Lynn, all he could think was that it should be Paige in his arms instead.

Christian was still trying to work out what had gone so suddenly wrong. Had she really been that concerned about him being an actor? And had she truly believed that he would eventually leave her, just because of what he did for a living? As it was, even dancing with another woman felt almost like a betrayal.

"Christian." He was pulled out of his thoughts by Lynn's voice. "You just stepped on my foot."

"I'm sorry." He took a step back, away from Lynn's feet. "Are you okay?"

"I'm fine, but since you're the one who has been missing steps all afternoon, I've got to ask—are *you* okay?"

If he'd learned anything during his time as a celebrity, it was to hold his cards close to his chest, because you never knew when someone would go running to the press. But when it came to his feelings for Paige, he had nothing to hide. Not from himself, or anyone else.

"I'm in love with Paige Walker."

"Well, in that case," Lynn said, looking not at all surprised by what he'd just blurted out, "I figured you've got two choices here. And believe me, after three husbands I know what I'm talking about. Option one, you go out, get very drunk, find another beautiful woman, and forget all about ever having known Paige."

"No." He couldn't even stand the thought of it. "That's not going to happen."

"I had a feeling we'd be getting right to option two, which is that you need to stop moping around my dance studio and do whatever you need to do to get her back." She walked over to the door and picked up her bag. "I'll go pick us up some smoothies down the street to give you some time alone to think."

With that, she walked out of the studio, leaving Christian to focus on his plan to not only get Paige back...but to persuade her to stay with him forever.

A vision of a romantic dance number from *Shall We Dance* started to quickly take shape in Christian's imagination, complete with costumes, sets, and extras. He would need help from Paige's sisters to get her to the right place at the right time and in costume. But since he knew they only wanted her to be happy—and he was almost certain that he did, in fact, make Paige happy—he hoped they would be happy to help out.

He could already see how it would go. Paige would walk in, and all the extras would be in their places. He would hold out his hand to her, and she would take it. They would dance together—another perfect dance—and at the end of it, he would tell her how much he loved her. And then, if he was really lucky, she would say she loved him, too, and together they would find a way to work things out.

"So, have you figured out a way to get her back yet?"

Christian looked up, surprised to see Lynn standing in front of him again. He had no idea how long she'd been gone. "I hope so."

"Just to be on the safe side, why don't you run all these great romantic plans of yours by me?"

Considering that he was probably going to need Lynn's help to choreograph the dance, he was happy to tell her his plans. The more he went on, the more she stared at him, wide-eyed.

"Wow. With something on the scale you're planning, I imagine she's going to be so swept up that she'll agree to just about *anything* you want."

Swept up. They were the two words he really didn't want to hear. That was what Paige had said right before she broke up with him. She'd said that when she was around him, she always got so swept up that she couldn't think clearly about what was real.

"It isn't going to work," he said as his grand plan came crashing down around him.

"You're kidding, right? Because it sure would work for every woman I know."

"Paige isn't like anyone else. She's not interested in my fame or money or anything like that. So if I go in there with a big Hollywood song-and-dance routine, she'll probably be even more convinced we don't belong together."

Lynn frowned. "So now what?"

"Somehow, someway, I need to find the right way to get through to her. A way to show her—"

"Show her what? That you aren't a star anymore? Because that certainly isn't going to happen any time soon. Especially not after this movie comes out."

Christian stopped dead. That was it, wasn't

it? There was only one way he was going to be able to convince Paige that he was more serious about her than he was about anything else. He needed to walk away from it all.

He needed to stop being a celebrity.

"You've nailed it, Lynn," Christian said. "I need to talk to my agent."

She looked at him blankly for a moment before the penny dropped. "Have you gone mad? You aren't seriously thinking about giving up your career for a woman, are you?"

"I will do whatever I need to do to be with Paige. And if that means walking away from the limelight, it isn't even a choice."

"You've got to be kidding me." She looked positively stunned. "Wait, you're not also thinking about pulling out of *Shall We Dance*, are you? Because there's a whole movie depending on you."

"We both know that I'm no more than a serviceable dancer. There are plenty of actors who could take my place."

"What about the gala?"

She had him there. When it came to the charity, there was no way he could just walk away.

"You're right. I'll do the dance tonight. But first thing tomorrow, I am calling my agent."

"Just promise me that you won't do it before then," she insisted. "That will give me a little time, at least, to try to talk you out of it."

If it meant he'd have a chance of getting Paige

back, no one would be able to talk him out of it. Still, he had a feeling Lynn wouldn't let go of it until he said, "I promise."

"Good. Now get back out on the dance floor. Because while I suppose torpedoing your career for a woman is kind of romantic, that means tonight is your last performance, so you are going to give them a show so great they'll think that you're Fred Astaire, Gene Kelly, and Nureyev rolled into one. I just hope Paige Walker is worth all this."

Paige was more than worth it. Christian would have done this a hundred times over for her and—

"Hey, we don't have any time for you to go back into dreamland!" Lynn said, all-business choreographer once again. "It's time to dance, lover boy."

CHAPTER TWENTY

The venue for the event was bigger than Paige had imagined it would be. A lot bigger. They'd taken the ballroom of one of LA's biggest hotels, and though there were tables set around the walls, they'd left plenty of space in the center for the performance.

At one point she was supposed to have been dancing with Christian in the middle of the ballroom. But now, she couldn't even get past the front door.

"I'm sorry." The security guard at the door was wearing a tuxedo, but he still did a credible impression of a brick wall. "If you don't have an invitation, you aren't coming in."

"But I need to see Christian Greer."

"You and every other woman here. Just because you have a nice dress on, doesn't mean I'm going to let you in." She'd borrowed a shimmering gown from Morgan that had clearly been designed with premieres in mind, stowing it in her carry-on for the flight to LA and putting it on in the bathroom of the hotel. "I'm going to have to ask you to move away from the door now, ma'am."

Paige could have tried to call Christian, but she needed to be able to see his face and look into his eyes when she told him she was sorry...and that she loved him. *Loved* him with all her heart.

For a moment, she considered telling the bodyguard that he was standing in the way of true love. But she could guess how that would go down. With loud, unstoppable laughter.

And then, likely, security guards escorting her out.

No, she definitely wasn't going to get through the door to the ballroom without some serious help. What Paige needed right now was—

Lynn!

She spotted the choreographer, who was wearing an elegant floral-print dress and long gloves, as she moved toward another door farther down a hall marked Employees Only. Paige ran to catch up to her, thankful for her years of dancing in heels so that she could easily run in them, too.

"Lynn, wait!"

The choreographer turned around and arched an eyebrow. "What are you doing here, Paige?"

The force of her words took Paige aback. "I—"

"Walked away, abandoning Christian when

he needed you," Lynn finished for her. "And then he made the crazy decision that he needs to give up his career to get you back!"

Paige felt her jaw drop, actually fall open. Somehow, she managed to form the words, "He's planning to do that? For me?"

"Right after the charity event tonight. Knowing him, he'll probably announce it on live television. Which I'm sure is intended to be so incredibly romantic that you'll agree to take him back, but you know as well as I do how much he loves acting. It would be a terrible mistake."

Paige knew how excited Christian got whenever he was talking about the movie business. And she'd seen how natural he was when he'd been acting his way through their dances. Plus, he was amazing with his fans. He was *meant* to be a star.

And yet, he was prepared to give all that up, just for her?

"We have to stop him," Paige insisted.

"We?"

"I would never want Christian to give up everything he loves for me. I love him. All of him. Exactly the way he is. I made a mistake, a terrible mistake, when I walked away from him. Please, Lynn, will you help me?"

The choreographer paused, appearing to consider the request. Somewhere in the background, Paige could hear music starting up. Lynn seemed to hear it, too, because she winced.

She gave Paige a stern look. "Are you

completely, one hundred percent serious about loving him?"

"I am."

"And you're not just going to freak out and change your mind again tomorrow?"

"No, I promise I won't. I love him. Not just today, but forever."

"And you already know how to dance with him, obviously."

"You saw us yourself."

"And you'd do absolutely anything to tell him everything you just told me?"

"Yes!"

"Then come with me."

As Lynn led the way through the employees-only door, she muttered, "At least we don't have to worry about your dress and makeup, since you came ready for the occasion." The next thing Paige knew, Lynn was opening a door and pushing her through. "Good luck."

Suddenly, Paige was under what seemed like a million spotlights. There were tables spread out around her, mirrors on the wall. Strangers occupied every one of those tables, their eyes on her with laser focus as she stood there, stunned. TV cameras were out in force, as well, to capture the celebrity-filled charity event.

Anywhere else, any other time, she would have frozen, then run back through the door she'd just come through. But tonight, Christian was right in front of her, looking more handsome and wonderful than ever, and instead of panicking, all she could feel was love. Pure, sweet love.

The look of sheer surprise on his face told Paige just how little he'd been expecting to see her. But as the music began, he lifted his hand and looked back at her with so much love that it was easy for Paige to forget everything but him.

She moved forward, taking his hand, letting him pull her close. She didn't know the routine for the dance Lynn had choreographed for them, but as Christian moved her into the first steps, it didn't matter. He led and she followed, the two of them moving effortlessly—and perfectly—together.

"I love you." She couldn't wait any longer. She had to tell him now. In the middle of the dance. In front of everyone.

"I love you, too." He swung her around, then brought her close again. "But coming out here, dancing with me in front of so many people and all the cameras...I thought this wasn't what you wanted. I thought you would never want to be with a man like me."

She pressed her cheek to his as they moved as one on the dance floor. "Lynn said you were going to give up everything for me."

"In a heartbeat, if that's what it takes for us to be together."

"No," Paige said as they shifted through a series of rising and falling turns. She was breathless by the time he brought her up against his body again, close enough to tell him, "Don't you dare give up your dream and everything you've worked so hard to achieve for me. You're right that I never thought I could be with someone famous, but you've made me rethink everything, Christian. *Love* has made me rethink everything. Together, we'll find a way to make it work for both of us."

And it would work, Paige was certain of it. Because whatever it took to make that happen, they would find a way to do it. She'd been so scared that he would choose Hollywood over her that she hadn't been willing to take a chance, and she'd been frightened of being in the spotlight, too. Yet now here she was dancing in front of a room full of complete strangers just to be close to him—and he had been willing to give up everything to be close to her.

Slowly, Paige became aware that he had taken her on her final spin. And when their dance was over, she stood by his side, her hand in his as they bowed, the applause breaking over them in waves.

Standing in front of an adoring audience was where Christian was meant to be, and she now realized that it was where she was meant to be, too. Right by his side, never letting him go.

"It looks like they're impressed by your dancing," Paige whispered to him. "I think this movie of yours might be a success after all."

"Even though there's only one Fred Astaire?"

Paige's hand tightened on his slightly. "I'm pretty sure there's only one Christian Greer, too."

"Ladies and gentlemen!" the voice of the

master of ceremonies boomed out through the speakers. "It's nearly midnight, so if there's someone you plan on spending the next year with, get ready to kiss them for luck in the year ahead."

It felt perfect and oh-so-right when Christian pulled her close again. Even so, she knew she had to ask, "Are you sure?"

"I've never been more sure about anything, or anyone, in my entire life. Are you sure that you aren't just getting swept up by me again?"

"There's no question that you are irresistible," Paige said with a sweetly seductive smile meant only for him, "but I'm here because I love you. And even if I am getting a little swept up tonight by my amazing dance partner...well, there's no one else I'd rather get swept up with." She knew now, without a shadow of a doubt, that he wasn't going to leave her. And she was never going to leave him.

Regardless of wherever life led them, they'd go together.

The countdown quickly went from ten to one, and as soon as the words *Happy New Year* rang out, Christian kissed her. Around them, as people cheered or kissed partners of their own, Paige's world came down to one man.

The man of her dreams.

Her mouth danced against Christian's as eagerly as she'd danced with him. And when they both finally came up for air, the crowd was still celebrating, clinking glasses and toasting the New

Year...with cameras recording it all.

"This is going to be all over the entertainment news, isn't it?" she said. "I'll probably have thousands of angry fans hunting me down for stealing away their heartthrob."

"I'm sure they'll think I'm one very lucky man," Christian said. "And you know, if you want to avoid the media attention, we should probably make a run for it."

"Do you have a secret hideaway in LA?"

"I was staying with my sister, but I was thinking that for tonight we could find a hotel room overlooking the beach." Christian's smile promised things that made Paige shiver in wonderful anticipation.

"I have to admit, I *do* like you in hotel rooms. Although I definitely want to meet your family, too."

"Tomorrow," Christian assured her. "We have plenty of time. In fact," he said as he pulled her close again and spun her into another dance, "we have a whole lifetime."

And as they danced together to the music that only they could hear, Paige knew she'd finally found the perfect partner she'd been waiting for her entire life.

EPILOGUE

The Walker family always got together on New Year's Eve to watch the big mirror ball drop in Times Square on TV. This year, however, their father had an iron grip on the remote. As a big fan of *Seattle General Medical*, he told them all that he wanted to watch the leading man take part in a New Year's Eve event in LA instead.

As she always did on New Year's Eve, Emily had prepared a huge selection of appetizers that everyone could nibble on throughout the evening. This year, she had chosen the theme of New Year's Around the World, with each appetizer representing a different country. Right now, it looked as if the Spanish tapas were going to be the first things to go, with the Japanese sushi a close second.

Everyone was still in a holiday mood, and they'd already played a rousing game of Pictionary. It was a big, warm, fun family evening, and Grams and Tres looked on with pride, as they did every year.

The only person missing tonight was Paige. She'd told them she had something important to do, but none of them knew exactly what it was. Of course, Emily had a pretty good idea that that *something* was connected to Christian Greer. But she kept her thoughts to herself for the time being.

Knowing that many of them would be leaving Walker Island in the morning to get back to their homes and jobs, their father did some last-minute catching up. "So, what plans does everyone have for this coming year?"

"I've got my last term at school starting next week," Hanna said, "and a couple of preliminary documentary ideas I want to finish putting together. Plus, Joel and I were talking about sailing down to Los Angeles at some point."

"Nicholas and Charlotte and I have the surfing tour in New Zealand and Indonesia," Rachel said. "We've also got some new curriculum materials for Charlotte, so we can keep up with her homeschooling. And we were talking about going climbing in Australia, too, if we can squeeze it in."

"You all know what I'll be doing this year," Morgan said with a smile. "Getting married!" She looked lovingly over at Brian, who looked as if he was ready to say *I do* right there and then.

In the space of one short year, three of her younger sisters had fallen head over heels in love and were now leading the fulfilling lives she'd always hoped for them. If their mother were still alive, Emily knew she would be so thrilled to see them settled.

"Your father and I are so proud of all of you," Grams said, "and we hope this next year is as wonderful as this year has been."

"Hear, hear!" they all called out, clinking glasses.

"And what about you, Emily?" her father asked. "Got any big plans for next year?"

The whole family stopped what they were doing and looked at her, including Michael, who, as an honorary Walker, had joined them for the evening. But before she could reply, Charlotte called out, "Look, Aunt Paige is on TV!"

For the next few minutes, all of them paid rapt attention as Paige danced with Christian. It was a beautiful dance, but the most beautiful thing of all was seeing how much the two of them clearly loved each other. And then, just a few moments after the dancing stopped, they started counting down to midnight. In the midst of the streamers and sparklers in the middle of the dance floor, they all watched as Paige and Christian kissed.

Emily was so happy for her sister, and her family were all cheering, too. They had all seen how perfect Paige and Christian were for one another when he was on the island learning to dance with her, and now it looked as if the happy couple had finally figured it out, too.

As Emily looked around the room, she saw that her other sisters were kissing the men they loved. She was *so* happy for them all, but she still couldn't help but wonder: When would it be her turn to fall in love?

Right then, she looked up and saw Michael standing in the doorway, staring directly at her as if he'd just made his own New Year's resolution.

One that—shockingly—seemed to include her.

~ THE END ~

ABOUT THE AUTHOR

When New York Times and USA Today bestseller Lucy Kevin released her first novel, SEATTLE GIRL, it became an instant bestseller. All of her subsequent sweet contemporary romances have been hits with readers as well, including WHEN IT'S LOVE (A Walker Island Romance, Book 3) which debuted at #1. Having been called "One of the top writers in America" by The Washington Post, she recently launched the very romantic Walker Island series. Lucy also writes contemporary romances as Bella Andre and her incredibly popular series about The Sullivans have been #1 bestsellers around the world, with more than 4 million books sold so far! If not behind her computer, you can find her swimming, hiking or laughing with her husband and two children. For a complete listing of books, as well as excerpts, contests, and to connect with Lucy please visit www.LucyKevin.com.

28193337R00112

Made in the USA
Lexington, KY
11 January 2019